All the
Winters
that Have
Been

OTHER TITLES BY EVAN MAXWELL

WRITING AS A. E. MAXWELL
Murder Hurts
Just Another Day in Paradise
The Frog and the Scorpion
Gatsby's Vineyard
Just Enough Light to Kill
The Art of Survival
Money Burns
The King of Nothing

WRITING AS ANN MAXWELL
The Ruby
The Secret Sisters
The Diamond Tiger

ALL THE WINTERS THAT HAVE BEEN

◇ ◇ ◇

EVAN MAXWELL

HarperCollins*Publishers*

HarperCollins books may be purchased for educational, business, or sales promotional use. For information please write: Special Markets Department, HarperCollins Publishers, Inc., 10 East 53rd Street, New York, NY 10022.

FIRST EDITION

Designed by Caitlin Daniels

Library of Congress Cataloging-in-Publication Data

Maxwell, Evan, 1943-
    All the winters that have been / by Evan Maxwell. — 1st ed.
      p. cm.
    ISBN 0-06-017633-4
    I. Title.
    PS3563.A8998A795 1995
    813'.54—dc20   94-44714

95 96 97 98 99 ❖/HC 10 9 8 7 6 5 4 3 2 1

For Ann, especially.

But also for Elizabeth, for Jayne and Amanda, for Stella, for Joan and Marlene, and for Suzanne.

They all know why.

PROLOGUE

Every life comes from a union of two other lives. Every human has two parents who connected, whether for a moment or a lifetime.

Some of those unions are peaceful and loving, some are a horrible mess, and some merely take a lifetime to untangle. I am the product of the last type.

My legal name is Josh Hartel. It was given to me by Ted Hartel, a man I loved as a father, a man who treated me as a son.

But Ted Hartel was not my biological father. I suspected that for some time, but I confirmed it several days ago. I will spend the rest of my life sorting out my reaction to it.

I am seated at a small table in a cabin on the slopes of Denali, the tallest mountain in North America. It is fall. The first breath of winter has driven the wolves and the ravens down from the higher elevations. I am here to see them one last time before I go back to the Lower Forty-Eight.

I also came here last week to conclude the earthly affairs of Helen Hartel, my mother. She was an artist and the wisest person I have ever known.

Among the personal effects I found was a photo album. I also found Dane Corvin's journal. He was a gifted writer and an honest one, but he took a secret with him to his grave.

Dane Corvin was my genetic father.

Dane and my mother were together for a relatively short time, yet they were involved with each other throughout their adult lives. Their connection was not always easy. There was much anger, even more pain. They had to live through their lives to make sense out of what happened.

Now I'm trying to do the same thing.

On the table in front of me is the collection of Mother's photographs. Beside it is Dane's journal, in which he recorded his thoughts. I have looked at the photos and read the journal. Now I will try to tell their story.

Every family has an album. This story will have to serve as theirs, and mine.

ONE

Dane Corvin watched the old man climb the steps for the last time. It would have been kinder to look away because Dewey Corvin made a hash of it. He grasped a cane with one hand and the railing with the other. He had to stop and pant on the first landing and the second. By the time he reached the top, he was trembling from exertion.

"Forty-one of those bastards," Dewey wheezed when he finally caught his breath. "They were a lot easier twenty years ago, when we built this place."

The old man glared at the offending stairs. Then he shook his head sadly.

"Been meaning to paint that railing for some time," he said. "Not enough days left now."

He drew a deep breath and stared down at the house through clouded and failing eyes. He didn't need to see the place, though. He had nailed every beam and rafter. He had split every shake in the cedar siding. He had cut and leaded every piece of stained glass in the brow windows under the eaves.

In his memory, Dewey knew the house better than most people know the backs of their own hands.

The colored glass in the brow windows caught the morning

sun. Dewey's eyes watered as he squinted against the brightness, or against something else.

"Twenty years," he said, more to himself than to Dane. "I had kind of hoped for more time. But I guess everyone does."

Dane stood beside the other man, wondering what to say. Finally, he laid his hand on Dewey's stooped shoulder. The old man's gnarled bones and twisted joint were like the dry limbs of an ancient fir tree.

Beneath his thumb, Dane could feel a knot on the end of Dewey's collarbone. It was an old injury. Dewey had torn up the shoulder working in the woods when he was twenty. Now he was eighty, and the mended fracture still pained him.

Dane squeezed gently, then lifted his hand.

"You sure you have to give up the house?" Dane asked softly. "Maybe we could put in one of those funicular railways, something to get you up and down the stairs. You could get somebody to come in once in a while to keep house. You could stay as long as you want."

Dewey looked at his nephew with sudden irritation. Dane was just over six feet tall and built like a middle-distance runner. He had a young man's dark hair. His dark beard was marked with a single striking blaze of white. He was tanned from a lifetime outdoors.

"What are you, Dane, forty-four? How would you know what old people need, what dying people want?"

A slow, bitter smile spread across Dane's face.

"I know a hell of a lot more about it than I did when I helped you build that house," Dane said. "We're all dying. Some of us are closer to the end than others, but we're all dying, inch by inch and day by day."

Dewey snorted with an old man's derision. "I suppose that's true, but you ought to wait till you're sixty or seventy before you start talking out loud about such things. It'll be more seemly with gray in your hair as well as your beard."

Dane looked out past the house through the dark green firs

to the water. The day was clear and clean. Puget Sound shone blue-gray and flat in a sun that still had a touch of summer's warmth to it.

A gull turned and soared, flashing white and gray in the sunlight. The bird called sharply, then wheeled and splashed into the water. Almost instantly, two more gulls glided in and landed beside the first. The three birds rocked together on the surface of the water, craning their necks to look down into the depths.

Dane understood the birds' behavior well. They had spotted a school of bait fish beneath the surface, fish driven up from the safety of the depths by a seal or a cruising salmon. Now the gulls floated overhead, waiting for the unseen predator to drive the herring within range of their cruel yellow beaks.

Dewey was right. It was easy for such speculations to seem flippant. Dane looked away from the power and peace of the open water, back to the man who was his father in every way that mattered.

"If I were you," Dane said in a low voice, "I wouldn't be in any rush to leave this house. When it comes to dying, this is as good a place as any, and a hell of a lot better than most."

The stooped old man caught a soft intensity in the younger man's voice. Dewey was surprised. He had never thought of Dane as anything but a youth.

Dewey's features softened. For a second, the tight mask that was cancer's mark dropped away, and Dewey became the gentle, whimsical man he once had been.

"It's better this way," Dewey said, patting Dane's forearm. "Winter's coming. I'm in no shape to feed the goddamned stove, much less to cut the five cords of wood I'd burn between now and spring."

"I'll cut it for you."

"No good, boy. I'm weak and I'm getting weaker. They say the surgery's only exploratory, but I have a feeling they won't like what they find. That's why I wanted to come back out here while I still have the strength, say good-bye to the place, put it behind me."

Dane wanted to protest, but he didn't.

"I want you to have the house," Dewey said. "You're the only one in the world who has ever really appreciated it . . . even if it's been quite a while since you were here."

Dane looked away, overwhelmed by Dewey's generosity and stung by the realization that he had not visited the house in twenty years.

He had been twenty-three when he and Dewey started the house, twenty-five when they finished it. Though Dane loved the place, he hadn't been inside it since.

Building the house had been an act of grieving and of affirmation for both men. Dane's parents—Dewey's brother and sister-in-law—had been dead for a year from a car crash. Uncle and nephew worked two summers framing and finishing the big wood and stone house on the steep lot just above the strait.

But that was not the reason Dane had never come back. Suddenly he needed to tell Dewey that.

"I've always appreciated what this house did for me," Dane said, looking at the house. "It taught me to build rather than to tear down."

Dane turned to his uncle. "I always appreciated what you did for me, too. That isn't why I stayed away. I guess I've just never been much for settling down."

Dewey shifted his grip on the curved head of the black cane in his hands.

"But you came back now," Dewey said. "Does that mean you're finally going to put down roots? Maybe get the government to transfer you out here and let you build a future rather than shipping you all over North America on a moment's notice?"

Dane shrugged, then shook his head.

"The Fish and Wildlife Service isn't interested in letting me settle down anywhere quite yet," Dane said. "They've offered me a new posting, a predator control project up in Alaska."

Dewey looked at Dane suspiciously. "Predator control? What sort of bureaucratic palaver is that?"

"It's a polite name for wolf killing. The sport hunters have finally convinced the government that wolves are the reason there's a shortage of trophy moose and caribou racks."

Dewey blinked in sudden outrage. "Wolves kill weak animals, not the trophy racks. Didn't anybody mention that?"

"I did, until I was blue in the face. The big shots disagreed. They decided somebody has to go in and wipe out three or four packs of the most handsome wolves you've ever seen. Then they decided that someone was me."

Dewey grunted. "Sounds like they want a meat hunter, not a wildlife biologist."

"Yeah. It's their way of punishing me."

"What for?"

"I was in Alaska last year on a very different job. I threw one of the governor's biggest contributors in jail up there. Politicians didn't like that. Now they're getting even. They'll make me eat a yard of two of shit, just so everyone else will understand that it isn't a good idea to put money men in jail."

Deliberately, Dewey spat over the railing. He had been a high school biology teacher and a summer park ranger–naturalist, as well as a carpenter. His gentle encouragement was one of the things that had pushed Dane into becoming a naturalist.

"You aren't going to do it, are you, boy?"

Dane shrugged. "It's that or a desk job in L.A."

"You wouldn't do well in a city. Too much of the wolf in you."

"Yeah."

"You going to quit?"

"I don't know." Dane smiled thinly. "Like Socrates, I have a choice of poisons. Unlike Socrates, I'm having a hell of a time deciding how I want to die."

Sighing, Dewey shifted his weight, leaning harder on the cane than he wanted to.

"Surprised you lasted as long as you did," Dewey said after a time. "Wolves make piss-poor bureaucrats."

Dane smiled, truly smiled. As long as the smile lasted, his hard features were those of a wolf, untamed and contented, fully alive, a creature blessed with the ability to live in the present rather than the past or the future.

"You sound happy about my outlaw status," Dane said.

Dewey laughed the dry, rustling laugh of an old man.

"Boy, if I thought you were a good federal employee, I wouldn't be giving you this house. I'd rather burn it to the ground than have some smug paper pusher putting curtains on the view."

Dane's laugh was deep and rich and strong. He circled his uncle's shoulders with a muscular arm.

"Tell you what," Dane said. "I'll look after the place for you for a couple of months. That's how much accumulated leave I have. I'll cut wood for you. By then, you'll be ready to come back and feed the stove yourself."

"It's not in the cards," Dewey said softly, shaking his head. "I won't be coming back. The house is yours to do with as you see fit. Maybe it will grow on you and you'll finally settle down."

"No," Dane said. "I have no more reason to settle down now than I did twenty years ago."

Something in Dane's tone made Dewey uneasy. He gave his nephew a long look.

"Is everything okay with you?" Dewey asked.

Dane hesitated, then shrugged. "As good as it gets these days."

Dewey waited for Dane to say more. Then the old man stared at his nephew in silent demand, trying to get beyond Dane's shell.

"I guess I'm just getting morose in my old age," Dane said. "It's not your problem. And in the long run, it doesn't matter anyway. No big deal."

Dewey sensed the surprising bleakness in Dane's tone again. He started to respond to it, but before he could speak, the pain bit him again, somewhere deep in his body. He flinched a little and drew a deep breath, fighting off nausea.

"Have it your way," Dewey said finally. "Just remember, a house goes downhill real fast if it's left vacant too long."

"I'll take care of the place, no matter what else happens. I've been thinking about taking early retirement in a few years. This would be a good place for that."

Suddenly, Dewey turned and looked down past the massive fieldstone chimney of the house and through the trees to the water beyond. When he spoke, his voice shook with emotion.

"Thank you, Dane. I appreciate knowing you'll have the house. I'd hate to think of some stranger in it while I'm still breathing.

"Afterward, I won't care, but not while I'm alive. Blood does count for some things, even in this screwed-up world. . . ."

His voice trailed off and he stared out through the trees to the water, seeking an excuse to delay the last good-bye. He could just see a blunt-nosed boat rocking on the water fifty yards offshore. A string of orange and white floats trailed out for three hundred yards in front of the boat, riding the outgoing tide.

"Gill netter," Dewey remarked.

Dane nodded. "Must be an Indian. Season's closed for everyone else."

"Say, that reminds me," Dewey said, brightening at having something else to talk about. "You remember that Indian girl you used to go out and see on the islands?"

Dane took the same kind of abrupt yet careful breath Dewey had, breathing around pain.

"She still lives out there," Dewey said. "Got married to one of those Alaska crab fishermen and had a family. I saw a piece in the paper about her son. He's off to Harvard, of all things."

Dane was silent for a moment. Then, reluctantly, he spoke the name of a past he had spent years trying to forget.

"Helen," he said softly. "Helen Raven. But she's not old enough to have a son at Harvard."

"Hell, boy, of course she is. Twenty years have gone by." Dewey chuckled.

"It doesn't seem that long."

"Nothing does, except to youngsters."

Dane nodded slowly, feeling a lot older, as though maybe he had been alive long enough to die, after all.

"She still lives out on the islands?" Dane asked.

Dewey nodded. "She's an artist. I cut the piece out of the paper, thought I'd send it to you. She's a widow now."

Dane gave his uncle a sideways look that was a mixture of anger and amusement and irritation.

"What are you driving at?" Dane asked. "You want my feet nailed to the ground before you die?"

Dewey hesitated, shifted his grip on the cane again, and sighed.

"Just an old man's notion. You sure spent a lot of time with her, back when we were building the house." He shrugged. "Roots aren't a bad thing to have."

For a long time, Dane said nothing. He stared off over the water through narrowed eyes. Then he drew a deep breath and blew through pursed lips, as though he were releasing some long-pent pressure.

"I'm off the marriage market," Dane said. "Now more than ever."

"Dyed-in-the-wool bachelor like me, huh?"

Dane shrugged.

"The woman I wanted wouldn't have me," Dewey said. "What's your excuse?"

Dane laughed curtly. "The same, but Helen had reason."

"Helen." Dewey took a careful breath. "Is she the reason you left and didn't come back?"

Silence was Dane's only answer.

It was all the answer Dewey needed. He drew another deep, cautious breath.

"Listen to me, boy. Dying makes a man look at things another way. Smarter. I'm dying, and I'm telling you what I've learned: You got anything to say to anybody, this woman or anybody else, you say it. No one, man or boy, knows his dying time. So get it done and get it behind you. The grave is too small for regrets."

Dewey looked once more at the house, then turned and shuffled away toward Dane's car in the driveway.

Dane stared out at the Indian gill netter's boat riding quietly on the water. The patterns of light and water, the sound of the wind, and the smell of the forest combined to unlock a memory Dane had spent twenty years forgetting.

TWO

The image was as clear as a good photograph. Dane could conjure it instantly and in every detail, down to the scent of the cedar tree beneath which he had stood.

Across the clearing, the girl lolled in the hot spring, comfortable as an otter. For a moment, he thought she was bathing nude. The steaming water covered her breasts, but moonlight gleamed on the smooth, wet skin of her shoulders.

Dane froze in cover like a wary young wolf, surprised by the girl's presence and astonished by her beauty.

Another form shifted in the shadows beside the pool. Waldo, a dark, brooding bear of an Indian, sat on a rock, waiting. The girl sculled quietly around the small, rock-lined pool, humming a song Dane didn't recognize. She said something to Waldo, but he didn't reply.

She laughed and moved her arms slowly, savoring the warmth of the pool. Then she splashed in Waldo's direction. The water of the pool swirled, revealing her body and then hiding it again.

Dane's breath caught in his throat. There was a perfection and a wildness about her, a freedom that he had never expected to see in any woman.

Silently, Dane cursed Waldo. The Indian was supposed to be alone. Poachers didn't conduct business in front of witnesses, particularly not in front of girlfriends. Fishing was men's business. So was selling three hundred pounds of illegal salmon.

Waldo slowly became aware of Dane's presence. He looked toward the edge of the clearing, directly at the cedar tree in whose shadow Dane stood.

"Come on in," Waldo called.

Dane stepped out into the moonlight but no farther. "You sure?"

"Yeah, sure, come on."

The girl said something softly, but again Waldo didn't reply. Dane moved slowly out into the moonlight.

As he approached the pool, Dane could feel the girl's eyes on him. He consciously avoided looking down at her. He didn't want to antagonize Waldo by ogling his skinny-dipping girlfriend, even accidentally.

But Dane could see her form clearly from the corner of his eye. Steam trailed lightly on the surface of the hot pool, as provocative as feather fans. He was still not sure whether the girl was dressed or naked.

"Nice night," he said to Waldo.

"Yeah," Waldo said.

There was a long silence, part of the ritual sniffing and testing. Dane let the silence roll on, waiting Waldo out.

"You want to swim or what?" Waldo finally said. He grinned slyly.

Dane allowed himself one uneasy glance toward the pool. The girl looked up at him. Moonlight gleamed in her clear, intelligent, almond-shaped eyes. A slight smile tugged at the corners of her generous mouth. She did not seem at all dismayed by the prospect of company.

The mists swirled a little, teasing him again. Moonlight glistened on the rising swell of her breasts. She sensed Dane's uneasiness but did nothing to allay it.

Dane drew a deep breath and tried to focus on Waldo.

"I didn't come here for a skinny-dipping session," Dane said.

"I came to talk some business, and I don't usually talk business in front of strangers."

Waldo chuckled. "That's not a stranger. That's my little sister, Helen."

The girl looked away, as though hearing her own name had made her bashful. She drew the water around her with her hands, scattering the mist and letting it gather again. She suddenly seemed younger than Dane had thought.

"Hi, Helen," Dane said, smiling at her as pleasantly as he could.

"Hi."

She met his glance for a moment, then slowly sank down in the water and tipped her head back. Her long dark hair spread out like a fan behind her head.

The girl's gesture was as alluring as a glimpse of skin beneath lace, all the more so because it seemed accidental. Dane's throat tightened. He had to look away to keep from staring.

"She may be your sister, but she's a stranger to me," Dane said curtly, impatient to get on with the deal.

Waldo chuckled again, enjoying Dane's uneasiness.

"Sure, sure," the Indian said. "No problem. Helen doesn't have to listen. I just wanted her to see you."

An alarm went off in Dane's head. "Why?"

"She's a witch. She can look right through people. She'll tell me if you have a federal badge in your boot."

Denying that truth had become a reflex to Dane. But now, when he turned to look at the girl, his defenses failed him. She was watching him carefully, looking right through him. He felt naked. He fought an impulse to flee that was close to panic.

The silence between them seemed to last all night. Dane stood his ground, staring at the girl in the water, waiting.

She lay back in the water again. Her hair fanned out as though on a pillow, and she watched him with her curious, knowing half-smile.

"He's a liar, Waldo," she finally said.

There was another long silence, almost as though all three of them were waiting for Dane to deny the accusation.

Abruptly, he bent down and picked up a handful of pebbles from the ground. He flung one into the dark shadows at the edge of the clearing.

"For Christ's sake, Waldo, cut the bullshit," Dane said. "Of course I'm a liar."

Dane fired another pebble into the darkness. It struck a boulder somewhere in the night and dropped to the ground.

"So are you," Dane added.

The third pebble snapped through the dense branches of the cedar.

"We all have to be liars and cheats, or we wouldn't be in this business," Dane said.

He threw the rest of the handful of pebbles into the trees with a quick snap of his wrist before he turned back to Waldo.

"Now that we've established our lack of character references," Dane said coolly, "let's get on with the deal. Or are you going to let your baby sister talk you out of five hundred bucks?"

With each word, Dane felt the girl's eyes on him. He turned and stared down at her, trying to bore through her innocence, daring her to repeat her charge.

Slowly, the half-smile left her face. Her eyes widened, her gaze deepened. Instead of seeing through him, she seemed to look into him all the way to his tarnished soul.

Dane was sure she knew the truth about him. He expected her to rise up out of the pool and denounce him.

Instead, the girl looked at him with dark, knowing eyes. Her quiet expression slowly transformed into a female smile that was half-invitation and half-challenge.

Then the smile vanished, as though Helen had just grasped the implications of what was happening between them. She broke the connection, looking past Dane into the glittering night sky. She drew a deep breath, as though trying to relax. But when she looked at Dane again, her composure was shattered.

For that moment, so was Dane's.

"Well, Helen, what do you think?" Waldo demanded.

"I don't know," she said.

Her voice said more. She was shaken and uncertain.

"Goddamn it, I need to know!" Waldo said. "Try again. Get up close this time."

Whatever Dane might think, it was clear that Waldo was convinced of his sister's abilities.

Helen came toward the edge of the pool, feeling for footing on the slippery rocks. Her eyes never left Dane's. Slowly, she emerged from the water.

She wore a swimsuit. It covered her body modestly enough, but it also accentuated the fullness of her breasts and hips and the entrancing narrowness of her waist.

Waldo is wrong, Dane thought. Helen is nobody's baby sister. She is a woman fully grown.

Helen came and stood in front of Dane. Her body steamed lightly in the cool night air. Like the night, her eyes were dark and alive.

"I can't tell," she finally said.

"What's wrong with you?" Waldo demanded.

"I . . . I have seen him somewhere before."

"Where?"

"In town, I guess. I don't know."

"So give me your best guess," Waldo said impatiently.

Helen gave her brother a long, enigmatic look.

"He is Wolf," she said. "I am Raven."

With that, she turned and walked back into the water. Dane and Waldo both watched her go. Only when she was submerged again did Dane feel able to draw a breath.

Helen swam until she was beyond overhearing whatever Dane and Waldo might do.

"Let's talk business, Mr. Las Vegas Hotshot," Waldo said. "But don't hand me that crap about five hundred bucks. The fish are worth a lot more."

Dane hid his relief and began bargaining. The harder he bargained, the more at ease Waldo became. They argued for twenty minutes before Dane finally agreed to pay two dollars a pound for the salmon. During that time, Waldo freely admitted that the fish had all been caught by Indian subsistence fishermen in gill nets. Not one of the salmon could legally be sold into the commercial market.

That admission was more important than the deal itself. It amounted to a confession of guilt. It was the real reason Dane was there in the first place.

Helen had been right. Dane was living a lie. He wasn't a Seattle fish buyer with shady connections to restaurants in Las Vegas casinos. He was a federal fisheries officer fresh from training, and he was working an undercover poaching investigation. His target was Waldo.

The tiny tape recorder in the small of Dane's back caught every word of the illicit deal. Dane was on the way to proving his first case in court, and Waldo was on his way to federal prison.

Dane's memory of that night was vivid, right down to the sharp guilt he felt, then and later. He didn't mind deceiving Waldo, who was using his status as an Indian subsistence fisherman as an excuse to catch and sell tons of fish on the illegal market.

Nor did Dane mind lying to other Indian fishermen involved in the scheme. Waldo wasn't alone in his illegal fish sales. A half-dozen men in the Indian village were doing the same thing.

The illegal fishermen used plastic gill nets and metal boats to plunder a resource that had fed their people for thousands of years, back to the time when fish were caught in bark nets and impaled on wooden spears. Dane had no qualms about lying to illegal fishermen to put them out of business.

But lying to Helen was a great deal more complicated. She was innocent, both in the criminal sense and in the human sense, but as time passed, Dane found himself drawn back to Raven Island more to see her than to gather evidence for his case.

Dane went to Raven Island alone, because it was impossible for backup agents to follow. Each time he went, he spent hours drinking and joking with Waldo and the other poachers. Then, at the end of the deals and the drinks and the bullshit, Dane would get up to leave, and Helen would appear, almost by magic, usually with a new drawing or carving to show him. They would look at each other and slip away together.

They walked together and talked about anything and everything except Waldo and illegal fish. They never touched, except by accident. They were as open as children, despite the single lie that was between them like a ticking bomb.

Dane tried to tell himself that the relationship gave credibility to his cover story. It gave him a reasonable excuse to hang around the village even longer, gathering information.

But he quit using that rationalization soon enough. The truth was that Helen drew him to her the way fire draws a wild wolf. She was intelligent and funny and attractive. She was naturally curious and genuinely open. She had a generous heart and a teasing spirit as wild as his own.

Dane had never been in love before. Now he had fallen for the one woman who could get him killed, if she chose to. At the time, the whole tangle had seemed inevitable.

But looking back on it from the distance of twenty years, he was astonished that he could have allowed it to happen.

Helen was half-Indian, which meant she didn't fit comfortably into the Scandinavian and redneck society of western Washington. But she didn't fit comfortably into the Indian village, since she was half-white.

Her mother was the daughter of a Winomish tribal leader, and her father was a Scots timber cruiser from British Columbia. After her father died, Helen's mother had married an Indian and returned to live with her family on the reservation.

For Helen, art was the common ground between her two cultures. Her paintings and sketches showed talent and great feeling. They also had an eerie depth that few artists achieve at any age. Helen had an artist's spontaneity, but even at twenty she had understood what she was trying to accomplish through her art: a synthesis of two conflicting heritages, Indian and Scots.

She sketched and painted birds and animals and landscapes like a traditional, representational white artist. Then she married the creatures with the totemic images and symbols from her Indian heritage.

The result was strong and clear-eyed. Her pictures were powerful and elemental, although they lacked the demonic quality of some totems. They captured both the substance and the spirit of the creatures in her world. They were creation in the purest sense.

That melding was important to Helen. She believed such amalgamation was the only way the world would ever create a better future for its peoples.

A different kind of melding took place between Dane and Helen. Dane was a scientist. His understanding of the natural world was detailed, factual, and objective. He knew the feeding, courtship, and nesting habits of crows and ravens, ducks and geese, eagles and hawks; when they migrated and where they fed. Helen, the artist, knew their totem stories, their mythic roles.

In the span of a month, their relationship began to lose its innocence. An electric kind of tension grew between them. Dane ignored it, telling himself that as long as he didn't touch Helen, his position as an impostor wasn't truly a betrayal.

Then one night, Helen surprised him. She was waiting at the edge of the clearing after Dane left the circle of poachers. Beneath her arm, she carried a warm wool blanket. Smiling like Eve, she took Dane's hand.

He told himself to pull back, but did not. He allowed her to lead him into a darkness scented by evergreen and ocean. Silently, they walked a hundred yards to a small meadow at the center of Raven Island.

Helen spread the blanket on a bed of ferns that she had prepared while Dane had talked to the other men. She dropped to her knees, reached up, and took Dane's hand in her own, drawing him onto the blanket with her.

Dane felt his legs go weak. Slowly, he sank down beside her. Their lips met in a kiss that was as new as fire and as old as man and woman. There was no hesitation, no fumbling. It was as though they had done this all before and would do it again until the end of time.

For a long, lost moment, Dane gave in to the magnetic power of this woman. Her mouth was soft. Her breath was sweet. She arched against him with a slow, insistent pressure that made him groan before he caught himself and drew back.

"You don't know . . . what you're doing," he said.

The words came haltingly. He was poised on the edge of passion. And disaster.

Helen touched his cheek with a shaking hand and smiled.

"I've never made love with a man, if that's what you mean," she agreed.

Dane's panic deepened.

"You're just used to white-girl virgins who won't say yes and can't say no," Helen said. "My mind is from my mother's side of the blanket. Indian women take the men they want."

She kissed him gently on the lips. "I haven't wanted any man until you, Dane."

The words and the kiss went through Dane like an electrical current. He was no virgin. He had done his share of fumbling and groaning in the back seats of cars with college girls his own age. He had liked it all, the heat and the movement, the pressure and the release. If what his partners said was any measure, he had gotten quite good at it.

But this wasn't just a matter of scratching a sweet kind of itch. What he felt for Helen wasn't sweet. It was fierce, as uncontrollable as a storm.

Dane moved toward Helen's warmth. He was powerless to stop. He kissed her again and again, until slowly, gently, they lay down together on the blanket. To make his hands quit shaking, Dane ran them lightly over her body, brushing the tips of her breasts and sliding down her ribs to her waist.

He spread his thumbs across her silk-soft belly and touched the tips of his fingers in the middle of her back. Gently, he pressed his thumbs into her. She moaned with pleasure. Her eyes closed, and she drew a deep breath, alive and moving beneath his hands.

"So this is what people do when they love each other," Helen whispered, eyes still closed and a tender, lazy, sensual smile on her lips. "No wonder they can't wait. So sweet."

"It isn't always like this," Dane said quietly. "Sometimes it's like this."

His hands slid down and cupped her rounded bottom. With quick strength, he drew her body beneath him and let his hips pin her to the ground. He was fully aroused and made no attempt to hide it. He straightened his body, thrust a bit, then again.

The effect was electrifying. For a moment, he thought they both would lose control. He gritted his teeth and lifted his weight from her. She arched against him, trying to maintain the contact.

"Don't stop," she said. "This is what we both were made for. *This.*"

Dane rolled to one side and drew one arm around Helen's shoulders, pulling her to him. His other hand brushed her breasts and then slid down to her waist. He stopped there, fighting himself, fighting her, fighting the fate that had made him come to her an impostor. It was a moment for truth, if ever there was one.

"Do you remember when we first met?" Dane asked roughly.

"Of course."

"Then you know I'm a liar."

"Do I?"

"How can you want me?" he asked softly, but clearly. "You aren't the kind of woman who could love a liar."

Helen's eyes flickered open. She looked at him with deep, quiet intensity.

"All of us have lies and secrets," she whispered. "I knew you were mine the moment you walked out of the forest."

"Is that why you didn't tell Waldo the truth?"

"I told him the truth that mattered. I did see you once, wolf to my raven."

"I would have remembered you."

"Only if you had dreamed with me. I was lying on a blanket with the smell of crushed ferns around me and a night sky above and a man by my side. It was my first time with a man. The man was you, Dane. The dream was four years ago."

As Helen spoke, she shifted his hand from her waist. With trembling fingers and a small smile, she undid the top two buttons of her blouse. Beneath the thin cloth, she was naked. She took his hand and laid it palm-down on her left breast.

Immediately, Dane felt the nipple stir and draw up like a small tongue licking his palm. Then, just beneath the soft, living flesh, he felt her heart beating; a deep, steady, strong rhythm that thrilled him like nothing he had ever felt before.

"My body and my heart and my dream all say your lies are not important," she whispered. "My body and my heart and my dream all say I must have you or I will die. Please, don't let me die."

Dane stared down at her gentle, confident, smiling face. Her love was there, as honest and direct as life itself, a gift from a girl-woman who dreamed. He could no more resist Helen than he could resist drawing a breath. To tell her all of the truth would have been to crush her heart beneath his hand.

Perhaps she was right. There are lies, then there are important lies. He caressed the softness of her breast. Then he told her the one truth that mattered.

"I love you," Dane whispered. "Whatever else happens, I love you."

Wrapped in the rough wool blanket against the chill of reality, Dane and Helen made love until morning. They parted in the dawn, smiling and light-headed from loving. Neither of them mentioned the future. Neither of them mentioned the past. There was only the moment, and they lived in it as fully as any two people ever had.

A week later, a federal grand jury in Seattle returned indictments against Waldo and half the men of Raven Island.

THREE

Seven days after moving into Dewey's house, on the morning of his forty-fifth birthday, Dane Corvin awoke from a dream of wolves. Rolling over in bed, he looked out at the new day. The first light of dawn spread across the dark waters of the sound like a blessing. A wing of pelagic cormorants lifted off a rock reef and flew in a low chevron formation down the channel toward Deception Pass. It was the seventh consecutive cloudless autumn dawn.

Dane felt the tension between living and dying most sharply on these early mornings. It was a good day to be alive, a hard day to be middle-aged with a clear appreciation of one's own mortality, and an even harder day to see Dewey's end rushing toward him.

I've slept in a dying man's bed, Dane thought.

Dewey seemed to be slipping fast, as though he had let go of his stranglehold on life after Dane brought him to the house to say good-bye.

Dane had always been a bit of a fatalist. Living and working with animals in the wild regularly reminded a man of the fragile nature of life. On the other hand, the certainty of death gave life a vivid edge. Dane had come to appreciate the wisdom of the Bushido code; he had learned to live like a soldier in battle, expecting to die at any moment and enjoying life all the more because of it.

He had also learned to let an understanding of death clarify choices for him. That was what the dream was about, a clarification of a choice he hadn't been able to put into words.

The dream had come to him several times in the past week. It always took more or less the same form. A pack of wolves watched him from the edge of a woods somewhere in the wild. They were curious, not threatening. They were waiting for him. They would have come to him, stiff-legged and wary, if he had called them.

Or, if they had called to him, he would have gone to them in that same cautious, curious, stiff-legged way.

Then, in his dream, he heard the sound of an approaching plane, small and low to the ground. The wolves recognized the sound, too. They had been hunted from planes before. They circled nervously, preparing to flee.

But instead of disappearing into the dark woods, the wolves lingered a moment, watching him. As the sound of the plane grew louder, the entire pack broke cover and dashed into the open, heading for him.

Dane could see the plane now. He could hear it start its low, lazy circle, angling for shooting position. Yet the wolves kept coming straight into the clearing. Straight to him. Did they expect him to protect them? Did they want him to flee with them?

Or did they simply intend to make a last stand beside one of their own kind?

In the cool light of the new morning, the dream seemed so direct and simple that Dane smiled. He had resolved his professional dilemma. He would take the posting to Alaska. But he wouldn't become a wolf killer. If he was in charge of the eradication program, he would be able to stall the process for months, perhaps years.

He might even be able to sabotage the program until the political climate changed and wolves were valued once again.

There were a thousand things a man could do, even if he was

being watched. There were a thousand time-consuming little bureaucratic battles that could be fought, particularly by a man who had nothing to lose, no career to protect, no expectations to fulfill.

Stretching, smiling, Dane decided that a clear sense of mortality conferred a bizarre blessing on mornings like this. An acceptance of eventual death was liberating. It gave a man the fierce freedom that one who fears dying can never experience.

There were still gaps in Dane's crystallizing plan. One was Dewey. Watching the old man and his doctors negotiate with death had been difficult. It promised only to get worse.

Dewey had spent the last week in the hospital. The proposed surgery had been rescheduled twice and finally postponed. Dewey simply wasn't strong enough. Now the doctors were trying to decide whether to hold him in the hospital or warehouse him in the nursing home next door.

Dane wished his uncle had not moved out of his house in the first place. Dewey would have had another week of autumn grace, of watching the strait change with tide and light, instead of seven sterile days and nights walled up in a hospital, waiting for anesthesia and pain or simple death. Moreover, Dane would not have been saddled with the obligation of the house. It tied him down at exactly the moment he wanted to act on his newly recognized freedom to help wolves.

With a silent curse, Dane lay back beneath the down comforter and stared up at the ceiling of the big bedroom, trying to think of a solution. The rich grain and the knots of the redwood planks that covered the ceiling came alive in the morning light. Dane remembered piecing the ceiling together with Dewey. The old bachelor had lavished a lot of attention on the wood, matching and fitting the planks as though they were a jigsaw puzzle.

"I'm single, and I'm not likely to change," Dewey had said. "I may as well have something interesting to look at while I'm in bed."

Dane had never been more grateful for his own bachelorhood.

After the doomed affair with Helen Raven, he had never come close to loving a woman. That was just as well, considering how his life was turning out. The responsibility of a wife and children would have complicated his choices incredibly. But he was free, nothing undone and no regrets.

Except Helen.

He had thought a lot about her in the last week. Her name appeared often on the pages of the journal he wrote in when he was troubled or restless, haunted by questions that had no answers. Dewey's two-month-old newspaper clipping had provided the catalyst. Dane had read the piece several times, fascinated as much by what the generic prose left out as by what it said.

> Josh Hartel, a Townsend High School athlete and scholar, has become the first local boy in recent history to be accepted on full scholarship at Harvard University in the East.
>
> Josh, the son of island artist Helen Hartel, will be departing this week for Boston.
>
> A starting basketball player for Townsend High and a cross-country runner with several high school records to his credit, Josh was also valedictorian of his class and a member of the National Honor Society. He expects to study art and photography at the eastern school.
>
> He is the son of Ted Hartel, a local fisherman who died along with seven other men when their crab boat went down in the Bering Sea six years ago.
>
> Mrs. Hartel is a painter, sculptor, and jewelry maker whose work has been shown in Seattle and Los Angeles. She is the granddaughter of Horace Raven, an elder of the Winomish Tribe and a lifelong resident of the islands.
>
> "Harvard is a long way off, and I'll miss him very, very much," his mother said, "but this is the chance of a lifetime, and he has to take it."

An artist, a mother, and a realist, Dane thought. What an odd and hopeful combination.

The rest of the article made it clear that Helen Raven had created a remarkable life for herself. Married to a fisherman and widowed before she was forty. Not a surprise, considering the mortality rate of fishermen on the Bering Sea. She had never remarried. Now she was an independent woman, a well-known artist, and the mother of a bright, successful son.

The clipping left Dane with an odd, disjointed feeling. He would have liked a photograph. He wanted to see how Helen had weathered the years between the dream of the fern bed and the cold reality of betrayal.

He had only seen her once since the night they made love in the forest. She had stood in a hallway in the federal courthouse, waiting for Waldo's arraignment. Her face grew still and cold as Dane approached. The expression on it chilled him. For all her youth, in that moment she was as old as love and betrayal. When he started to speak, she cut him off.

"I dreamed I was raven to your wolf," Helen said. "I was wrong. Go, wolf. Find your raven, or you will die before you ever live."

Then she turned and walked away without looking back.

The words Helen spoke were a riddle to Dane, but he couldn't ask for an explanation. The dark rage and despair he had seen in her eyes beggared any words he knew.

In the beginning, he had tried several times to see her again. The last time was a year after the trial. He had gone to the village and had been met with silent stares and unvoiced threats. Finally, a toothless old woman had looked up from her work by a fire.

"She is not here," the old woman said.

"I know she is here," Dane lied. "Someone saw her."

"They were mistaken. The one you knew as Helen Raven is dead."

Dane's body turned cold. "I don't believe you!"

The woman turned her back as though Dane no longer existed. The denial of his life was chilling. Then he realized what the woman meant. There was no going back. His lies had killed the girl he knew as Helen Raven.

At least, that was what Dane had decided twenty years before. Now he wondered if it might not be possible to make a mature Helen Raven understand what a girl could not. His betrayal hadn't been of her. His love hadn't been a lie. If she listened to him, and believed him, perhaps he would finally be at peace with himself.

Dewey was right. The grave was too small for regrets.

The rational part of Dane's mind pointed out that meeting Helen might increase his regrets rather than reduce them. They both had lived twenty years without resolution. Trying to force one now could wreck whatever peace either of them had achieved.

Yet the prospect of seeing Helen and of saying the things he should have said before was so alluring that Dane could not drive it from his mind.

Out over the waters of Puget Sound, white and gray gulls wheeled and cried above the sea, waiting for seals or diving birds to drive bait fish to the surface. The daily ritual of eating and being eaten had begun anew.

One day past. One day ahead. One less to go.

Dane's hand was on the covers, ready to fling them aside, when he heard a faint noise above him.

Thump. Scuff.

The sounds were faint, furtive, like rats in the attic. Dane tilted his head, trying to hear the sounds more clearly.

Rustle, scuff. Caw.

The box springs creaked coldly as Dane sat up in the old bed and slid out from beneath the comforter. The wood floor was covered with a handsome rag rug, cool to his feet. The floor itself was cold.

Thump, rustle. Caw, caw. Thumpity-thump.

Dane looked at his clothes thrown across the chair beside the bed and decided he would make too much noise getting dressed.

He slowly turned the knob on the narrow oak door that led to the attic stairs.

The cold wood of the stair treads popped dryly as Dane climbed. He shifted his weight to the outside of the steps, taking them two at a time, his bare shoulders brushing against the narrow walls of the stairwell.

The small dormer was set halfway up the steep roof of the house. Dane remembered the heady sensation of walking across the bright new fir rafters to install the window. The view was lordly and isolated.

Thump, rustle. Scuffle, thump.

As Dane reached the dormer, he could see a sleek, jet-black crow hopping across the cedar shakes of the roof. Then he heard the sound again.

Soft pecking noises. A crow's breakfast.

The bird pecked earnestly at a bunch of rust-colored madrone berries it held fast to the shakes with one crooked foot. The crow had its back to the window, so it didn't notice Dane.

Suddenly a dark shadow passed across the roof. A black raven swept past on outstretched wings that were half again as big as a crow's, half again as black, half again as shiny. The raven circled and dropped onto the shingles.

The crow looked up irritably, cawed a harsh lack of welcome, and went back to pecking at the berries. The raven ruffled her feathers and perched on the crown of the roof as though to deny any interest in the food. But she watched the madrone berries with a covetous eye.

Dane felt a stirring of excitement as he watched. Of all the birds he had studied, ravens had most intrigued him. All ravens were special. All ravens were She, fascinating and mysterious.

This raven was unaware of Dane. She was entirely focused on the madrone berries. Never mind that there were a dozen trees close to hand, and each of them was covered with berries. The raven wanted the crow's breakfast. She padded down off the crown of the roof, adjusting automatically to the steep pitch.

The crow looked up and clucked a warning like a nervous hen. It picked up the half-eaten bunch of berries and hopped a foot away, then put the clump down and went back to pecking.

The raven is Big Sister, Dane remembered. The raven and her little sisters, the crows. No one knows why the raven teases the crows. No one knows the ways of the raven. Perhaps not even the raven.

The words came back in Helen's soft voice. Helen Raven, just as lustrous and enigmatic as the feathers of this bird on the roof. She loved to tease. She loved to play the mysterious game of man and woman. She was an enigma, and then, for a moment, she was as direct as life itself.

The raven gronked unhappily, as though disappointed in her greedy little sister. She hopped once, then again, landing lightly on both feet. Then she rocked back and forth, eyeing the berries and plotting her approach.

The crow pecked at the berries, spraying the soft pulp with its beak. One of the berries broke off its stem and rolled toward the edge of the roof.

The raven was quick. She hopped to the berry and pecked at it before the crow could gather it in. The berry skipped a few inches, and the raven lunged again, almost forgetting the steepness of the perch.

The berry skittered another few inches before it wedged in a crack between shingles. The raven finally pinched it in her bill and gulped it down. Then she rocked back on her heels and resumed watching the crow, who was hunched over, protecting the madrone berries and feeding at the same time.

The raven had the advantage of size. She hopped closer and stared earnestly at the berries, too polite to demand but too intent to be ignored. The crow ate quickly, trying to finish the bunch and the disagreement at the same time.

The raven hopped closer. Now she was a foot from the crow. She made a low noise in her throat and shook her head from side to side, muttering to herself about ill-mannered younger siblings.

The raven's expression was so human and comical that Dane laughed out loud. Both birds heard him at the same time. The crow bolted, abandoning the stem and the remaining berries. The raven looked up gravely, regarding the naked man in the dormer window as though he were a fellow conspirator. Then she hopped over and finished the crow's breakfast.

When the raven was done, she gronked a polite thanks, hopped to the edge of the roof, and dropped off like a black leaf caught in the wind. Returned to her natural element, the raven wheeled regally, catching the first updraft at the edge of the cliff. Spreading the five flight primaries on the end of each wing like slender, elegant fingers, she hung in the wind, looking back at Dane.

When she was sure he was watching, she twisted her body so that the first direct rays of sun flowed across the feathers of her back. The light shifted, the feathers caught fire, and the black raven became an incandescent silver-white shape.

The raven's unexpected, shattering beauty squeezed the breath out of Dane. She was power and magic, just as Helen had been the first time he saw her.

Witch, enchantress, lover, woman.

Then the raven turned in the light and was black again. With quick beats of her wings, she flew beyond Dane's sight, leaving him alone and aching.

Until that instant, Dane hadn't understood Helen's hold on him. For twenty years, he had lived a solitary life. He had known other women, had liked a few and enjoyed them all. But he had never loved, never married. He had always told himself that he was merely selfish, that he loved his freedom more than he loved any single woman. Now he knew differently.

He had not married because no woman had ever really stood a chance. All of them suffered in comparison with the impossible standard, the magical woman with the raven hair and the intelligent, enigmatic smile, the woman he could not win, the woman who would not have him, the woman he had never meant to hurt but whom he had hurt more than he believed possible.

In that instant Dane understood what Dewey had really meant. There was no grave on earth big enough to hold his regrets, because he would be there, cursing himself through all eternity.

FOUR

Helen Hartel was at her workbench when she felt the first breath of winter across her neck. The breeze off Orca Passage was always cool, but this morning autumn seemed well and truly launched. She glanced up from the wax form she was carving. The morning fire in the small stone hearth was still warm and bright.

Out of new habit, Helen's eyes moved to the picture on the mantel above the hearth. She thought of Josh, three thousand miles away in a New England autumn. Did he have his new coat? she thought. Did he have enough sense to go out and buy one?

No! Enough! He's nearly a man. He can decide whether he needs a coat. He's smart enough to get a scholarship to Harvard. Surely he's smart enough to know if he's cold.

Helen tried to avoid smothering her son. She had raised him to be his own person. She didn't need the acceptance committee at Harvard to tell her she had done a damned fine job.

But she had discovered in the last two months that the mother of a college student needed reflexes that were different from those of a high school parent. She had to remind herself to let go, lest she cripple her son with love and support. Josh was no longer merely hers. He belonged to the world. He was going to have to make his peace with it however he could.

Helen walked across the studio and looked more closely at the silver-framed picture on the mantel. She had many photos of her son, but this one was her favorite. It was a self-portrait, taken while he was perched on his favorite rock in front of the cabin, with his two pet ravens hunkered down on the rock beside him.

The sun had poured fully on the boy's dark, handsome face as he held the camera at arm's length, grinned directly into the lens, and tripped the shutter. The picture captured the intensity, the roiling energy, and the blinding good humor of a boy-becoming-man.

Josh had dark, thick hair, skin the color of magnificently tanned deerskin, and clean, strong features that were both Indian and European, like his mother's. But unlike Helen's, Josh's eyes were light, sometimes green, sometimes almost blue. They were striking, like a gentle wolf's. They were almost the only reason Helen ever thought of Dane Corvin any more.

Helen pushed the image of Dane away automatically. Ted Hartel had been a good man and a decent husband. They had lived together three or four months a year, when he was not in the Bering Sea, and they had enjoyed a measure of affection. But he had never been wolf to her raven.

Josh had been a month old when Helen married Hartel. The fisherman was fifteen years older and sterile; he had accepted the child as his own without question. Josh's patrimony was Helen's secret, one that she had lived with so long that it had almost lost its power to shake her.

Reluctantly, Helen looked away from the mantel and returned her attention to her workbench. She had been creating a brooch, a woman's face and torso she intended to cast in silver. The face would be edged with white bone carved to resemble locks of hair.

She had already picked out a pair of milky cabochon moonstones as breasts, but the features of the face had eluded her. She always strove to combine the pagan energy of Indian art with the sublime power that grew from Celtic culture. But now she wanted the brooch to be both continuation and departure from her theme.

For the first time in her career, Helen was using the human

form as the basis of her work. The change grew out of her own new condition. She was alone and utterly free for the first time in her life, and she wanted to express that freedom.

She was compelled by the female predicament, the woman's experience. The beginning of any woman's life, even an artist's, was taken up with externals. Woman was connected to man and child and home, whether she liked it or not. Helen understood that and accepted it.

But now, in the span of two months, Helen's condition had changed. She was free in a way that no active wife and mother could possibly be. She had no man, neither husband nor lover nor son, to encumber her. Now she could set out on her own journey, the journey of her own life.

She wanted the new piece to convey that freedom, so she had named it even before she carved the first wax. It would be called *Journey Woman.*

But naming a piece was different from executing it. All morning long, Helen had been trying to imagine the expression on *Journey Woman's* face. An idea was just taking form when the phone rang.

"Helen? This is Irene down at the gallery."

Irene Tensing ran the Sea Lion Gallery, the most expensive art gallery in Harbor Glen, at the other end of the island. Irene was a droll, round-faced Indian woman with a University of California degree in art history and the mercenary instincts of a Yankee trader. She was also Helen's chief patron, a major outlet for her work, and her principal, persistent critic.

"Hello, Irene, and yes, I'm still going to do *Journey Woman,* if that's what you're calling about, so don't try to talk me out of it," Helen warned instantly.

Like most gallery owners, Irene had reservations about artists who suddenly went off in new directions. Such departures usually made their old work hard to sell.

"That's not what I called about," Irene said. "Somebody was just in the gallery asking about you. A man."

Helen felt an uneasy twinge. She was a single woman whom men found attractive. As such, she had learned to be wary of strangers.

"I got rid of the only guy in my life weeks ago," Helen said crisply. "He went off to Harvard. I hope you told this one I didn't need another."

"I didn't realize he was even interested in you, at first. Mainly he wanted to know about your brother."

"Waldo?"

"Yeah, asked for him by name but didn't seem to want to say why. I thought he was a cop or something. He's definitely not local, too much polish for that. He was unusual, good-looking in a hard way."

"What did he want with Waldo?"

"He said it was a private matter. I told him Waldo wasn't around at the moment."

"Did he leave?"

"No. He started looking at the art. He really liked your *Wolf and Raven* but seemed to think it was a bit overpriced. 'Does she really get that much for a wood carving?' is what he said, like he didn't believe it."

Helen thought about the carving for the first time in years. It was a stylized assemblage, a bold, beautiful totemic raven perched on the branch of a tall cedar tree with a huge, fierce, yet somehow playful wolf peering up at the raven from behind the trunk.

The carving drew directly on Winomish legend. Wolves and ravens were said to hunt together and to cooperate secretly, despite their dissimilar natures. As a child, Helen had always loved the story. As an adult, she was still fascinated by the theme.

The *Wolf and Raven* had been the first of Helen's work Irene Tensing ever displayed, although its size, more than fifteen feet from top to bottom, made it unsalable. Irene continued to keep it in her gallery because she said it was still the best and most intriguing thing Helen had ever done.

Helen loved the piece, too, although now it seemed to her to have been executed in another, distant life.

"He's certainly not the first one to think my work is over-priced," Helen said, amused. Then her voice changed. "Did you tell him what happened to Waldo?"

"I didn't see any need to," Irene said. "I thought he might be a fed, and feds never did the Ravens any favors."

Twenty years rolled away in an instant, and Helen was a Raven again, caught up in the torment of Waldo's first brush with federal agents.

And her first brush with Dane.

Quickly, she glanced at the picture of Josh on the mantel. She tried to center herself on him as she had so many times in her life, telling herself that no matter the cost, no matter the pain, no matter the grief, it had all been worth it.

But Josh was gone now, grown, unaware of the secret of his wolf's eyes and lean, easy strength. He was gone, and she was left with the past she had never understood, only endured because there was no other choice.

"Helen?" Irene asked. "You still there?"

"Yes. Sorry."

"Thinking about Waldo?"

"Waldo, and Josh. Where does the time go?"

And why doesn't it take the pain of old mistakes with it? Helen added silently.

"Anyway, thanks," Helen added briskly. "The guy was probably just some old jailhouse pal of Waldo's looking for a free meal."

"He can put his knees under my table any time," Irene retorted. "He moved real nice."

"Then I'll send him along if he shows up here. God knows, there isn't room at my table."

Helen hung up the phone and gazed out through the large open windows to the dark blue water of the passage, trying for a moment to make sense of the stranger who had been asking questions about the Ravens. Someone looking for Waldo? Someone who didn't know Waldo died years and years ago? Her brother was long buried, as were all her unresolved feelings about the way he died.

Gradually, the serenity of the autumn day drew Helen back to the present. Fifty yards offshore, a small raft of hooded mergansers and harlequin ducks bobbed in the lapping waves. A skein of snow geese came in from the north and turned toward the marshy flats in the middle of the island.

The geese were the first migrants pushed south by the coming winter. They had summered and courted and mated and raised broods in the Arctic. Now they were headed for California and sunshine.

The freedom of the birds sent a shiver of recognition through Helen. Suddenly, she knew what she wanted for *Journey Woman.*

Helen picked up the wax form and began to carve, creating a woman with a raven's teasing, piercing awareness, and her deceptive stillness in the instant before she spreads her wings and leaps into the wild wind.

For almost an hour, Helen carved and smoothed and shaped the wax with her mind, her hands, and her knife. Finally, she laid the hooked craft blade aside and inspected the form that would eventually be replaced by silver in the molding process.

There was something familiar about the face. It took Helen a moment to realize that *Journey Woman* had her own eyes and some of her own features. But the carving was not a self-portrait. Instead, it was what Helen wished to be, an Everywoman who was shadowed, powerful, regal, complete in herself; and compelling because of it.

Helen laid the wax figure aside and only then realized that she was cold. The fire had died, and the wood box was empty. With a faint sigh of exasperation at the world's intrusion into her concentration, Helen drew on a sweater and went outside.

Clean straight rounds of yellow Douglas fir were scattered

haphazardly in the side yard, the four cords of wood she would need for the winter. Since Josh had turned twelve, he had been responsible for splitting the rounds into stove and fireplace size, but the job had been overlooked in his rush to go East. He had split part of a cord. Most of that was gone, as was the cedar kindling.

For the moment, Helen was making do, splitting a log or two at a time with a wedge and a sledgehammer and vowing to hire a lout with broad shoulders to work on the wood for her. She knew that her time was better spent at the workbench than at the woodpile.

On the other hand, it was nice not to depend on anyone for a change, not to have to rearrange her life around needs other than her own.

She picked up the short-handled ax and turned to the old cedar kindling stump that had been laid aside to dry. With a clean, easy stroke, she split off a slab the thickness of her thumb. As she picked up the flake of wood, she caught the clean, spicy scent of fresh-split cedar.

Holding the flake to her nose, she inhaled its fragrance. Then she studied the wood. It had an interesting whorl, like a cat's eye, in its center. The pattern was too intriguing to burn, so she set the flake aside, thinking she might carve something from it later.

She split off another piece of cedar, and then, gripping the ax like a hatchet, she positioned the flake to split it for kindling. But this flake, too, had lines of its own, a hidden life waiting to be revealed by a wood carver's knife.

The third flake was fascinating, too, and the fourth. Helen looked at the growing pile she had set aside and laughed out loud, remembering how Josh had teased her about her "someday pile." Still smiling, she raised the ax to break off another flake.

Suddenly, Helen sensed she was not alone. She stood and whirled around. She found herself face to face with a tall, rangy, good-looking man. He was dressed in jeans, a clean plaid shirt, and a handsome deerskin vest. He had dark hair and a dark beard with a single pale slash of silver. His eyes were those of a wolf, gold and green by turns.

Josh's eyes.

Dane Corvin's eyes.

"You wear the beard to show off the blaze," Helen said. "A bit of silver and you think you're all grown up."

Dane barely heard the words. He had come around the corner of the little cabin and found Helen laughing, her head thrown back, her breasts taut against the dark cloth of her blouse. Seeing her made his knees go weak with physical desire. He hadn't expected that.

Helen read his expression as she would read the evening sky at weather change. For a terrible instant, she was a girl again, floating in a black pool, watching her future walk toward her with a wolflike grace that made breathing impossible.

"It's been a long time," Dane said, an off-center smile on his face. "If I had known you'd have an ax in your hand, I might have let it be a day or two longer."

Helen stood frozen longer than she wanted to, remembering a foolish raven's faith and a wolf's raw power. Then she sank the head of the ax a solid two inches into the cedar stump and stepped back from it.

"Never would have been too soon to see you," Helen said. "Good-bye again, Dane."

"You have a right. But so do I. There are some things I have to say, to try to . . ." Dane's voice faded.

Cursing, Dane ran the fingers of his right hand through his hair.

Helen's heart turned over. Josh did the same thing, the same way, for the same reason: frustration.

"Damn!" Dane muttered. "Damn the words. I'm no damned good with them."

Helen closed her eyes so that she wouldn't see the son's vulnerability in the father.

"Go away," she said.

"Not until I explain. Let me try, Helen."

Her eyes opened as black as a raven's. She stared at Dane for a long moment. Then she looked past him, just as she had in the pool that night twenty years ago.

Without a word, Helen walked past Dane, heading for the cabin door.

He watched her, seeing her more clearly than he ever had. A younger man, a man without the chilling luxury of death in his bones, would have taken her silence as rejection.

Dane had done that once. Perhaps it had been a mistake. Perhaps it hadn't. Good or bad, right or wrong, walking away from Helen had brought no peace, only regrets.

Dane turned and followed Helen into the cabin.

He entered a second too late to see that she had removed a silver-framed photograph from the mantel and put it, facedown, in a drawer where she kept her most valuable creations.

The lock clicked into place as Helen turned to face Dane.

FIVE

Dane stood in the doorway and slowly looked around the cabin, as though he were trying to understand Helen from the materials that filled her daily life.

Helen glanced around the place herself, worried that Josh's photograph was not the only evidence that would betray her secret. The door to Josh's room was closed, but a glass jar of his favorite agates sat on the windowsill. They gleamed and glowed in the sunlight like rough gemstones, drawing her eye. Her heartbeat quickened in fear before she remembered that Dane had no way of knowing the agates were linked to Josh.

Helen's secrecy was instinctive. She had spent her entire adult life protecting the truth of her green-eyed son. Now she stood in front of the desk, her hip blocking the locked drawer, her arms folded stiffly across her breasts, waiting for Dane to break the silence.

"So you became an artist," he said quietly. "I often wondered."

"You already knew I was an artist. You think I'm paid too well."

Dane grinned slowly, understanding what had happened.

"I thought that woman in the gallery might call," he said. "She was pretty protective of you."

When he didn't mention the *Wolf and Raven,* Helen wondered whether Dane had even recognized its theme.

He moved into the room as though drawn to the jar of Josh's agates.

"How did you find out where I live?" Helen asked sharply, hoping to divert Dane.

He seemed surprised by her tone.

"County tax rolls," Dane said, turning away from the jar of stones. "Public records are good for something."

A chill ran down Helen's spine. Birth records were public, too. Dane's name was not on Josh's birth certificate, but neither was Ted Hartel's. Helen hadn't married him until Josh was a month old.

"So why did you bother Irene, if you already knew where to find me?" Helen asked. "Were you just snooping?"

Dane's easy grin vanished. The words cut deeply.

Helen felt a prick of unkind delight. It was nice to know that he could be wounded.

Without speaking, Dane moved around the rest of the room slowly, examining its details as an ornithologist examines the nest of a rare and interesting bird. He assessed the positioning of the easel and paint palette in the corner with the good light from the north and east windows. He looked over the workbench with its west light and its rank of tools and metal-working jigs on the wall beside it. The wood chisels were freshly sharpened and gleaming on their pegs, just an arm's length from the platform where Helen carved her cedar logs.

Helen followed Dane with her eyes, afraid that Josh's true parentage was somehow revealed by the room itself.

Dane picked up a chisel from the table and tested its sharp edge with the ball of his thumb. He nodded approvingly, then put the chisel back.

"I liked the piece in the gallery," he said. "I only remarked about the price because it would take me two months to make that much."

He glanced up and gave her a quick, self-effacing smile.

Helen felt a rising flush of irritation. She dropped her arms to her sides and straightened her shoulders.

"A piece like that takes several months to do, sometimes longer," she said. "I'm not getting rich, if that's what's bothering you."

Dane laid the chisel on the worktable and moved away. "Your boy's school must be costing you a bundle," he remarked.

The fear sprang up in Helen's throat again. "How did you know about my son?"

"Somebody showed me a piece out of the local paper. That's how I knew you were here on the island."

Helen drew a slow, deep breath, trying to loosen the bands of fear across her chest.

"If you saw the story, you know he's on scholarship," she said. She moved away from the desk to the worktable and picked up the chisel that Dane had inspected.

"I guess I did know that," Dane admitted. He sensed Helen's agitation, although he didn't understand its source. "You must be very proud of him."

"I am. He's very bright, and he has worked very hard."

She selected a sturdy cedar stake that was left over from a carving. Bracing the stake on the table, she began to turn feathers of kindling off it with the sharp end of the chisel.

Dane watched her carefully. At first, Helen thought the sharp tool made him uneasy. Then she realized he was looking at her hands. She suddenly saw them as a stranger would. The years and mishaps with the chisel and the craft knife had left a network of scuffs and small scars on her thumbs and fingers. She suspected Dane was judging them by how smooth they once had been.

She shot him a dark-eyed look that seemed a warning. Then she turned away and walked to the fireplace.

"You didn't come here to talk about art, nor did you come to talk about my son," Helen said, praying it was true. "Why did you come? Why now?"

"Curiosity."

The word sounded flippant and irritating. Helen pretended she hadn't noticed. She stared down at the fireplace for a moment, then slowly knelt and began to fuss with the ashes.

◇ 44 ◇

"I'm not sure I understand," she said. Her voice was deliberately calm.

"I was visiting my uncle, Dewey, over in town. He remembered that we knew each other and showed me a newspaper clipping about your boy going off to Harvard. The story got me to thinking. I wondered if twenty years was long enough."

"For what?"

Dane shoved his fists into the pockets of his light deerskin vest.

"The last time we saw each other, you talked riddles and I was struck dumb," he said. "I wondered if maybe we could speak to each other calmly after twenty years."

Helen didn't respond. Kneeling on the hearth, she felt the residual heat that was stored in the bricks, stronger and more vivid than it should have been. She suspected that the ashes from her first fire were still warm. She laid the shaved cedar stake on them.

"This is the first time you've been back," Helen said quietly. It was more an observation than a question.

"I tried to see you a couple of times, that first few months after the arrests, but you didn't want to see me. I had to worry a little about Waldo, too."

Helen looked at Dane sharply. "Why?"

"Didn't he ever tell you? I went up to the federal prison camp to see him after he was sentenced. He said he'd cut off my balls for crab bait if he saw me on the outside. Then he said he'd do even worse if I didn't leave you alone."

Helen looked back into the fire. "So that's why you stayed away?"

Dane hesitated. "I suppose I could use that as an excuse, but it would be a lie and I don't want to lie to you. We had enough of that twenty years ago.

"The truth is that I was a little scared, but not of Waldo. I was afraid you might do exactly what you're doing now, pretending that I'm some kind of unwelcome stranger."

"Of course you're a stranger. I don't even know your real name, not for sure."

Dane was silent for a moment. He swallowed hard, anger and something else.

"You always knew my name," he said. "I never lied about that."

Helen sat silently on her heels staring at the fire, refusing to respond.

"After the first year, I guess it was just easier to stay away than it was to come back," Dane finally said. "But now I had to. Dewey is sick and I'm his only blood kin. You never know how much blood means until it comes to dying. . . ." Dane ran his fingers though his hair again. "I had a little time coming from the government, so I came back."

"I'm sorry about your uncle," Helen said softly.

"So am I. All that's left of his life and dreams and blood is me. It goes both ways. I want to help him, but there's a limit to what the living can do for the dying."

Helen was touched by Dane's words, but she sought not to show it. She steadied her hand and reached for a sheet of newspaper from the stack beside the wood box. Before she could lay the paper beside the whittled cedar stake, a lingering brand in the ashes made the reddish wood begin to smoke.

Dane watched with fascination as Helen engaged in the ageless and elemental act of building a fire. Her kneeling position emphasized the curve of her hips. The denim of her jeans was soft and worn. It molded smoothly to the woman beneath. She reached for the last chunks of firewood in the box. The movement stretched her blouse across her breasts.

For an instant, the world seemed to stop. Dane watched Helen, transfixed by his own deep reaction. He was stunned, almost frightened. Helen still had a magical power over him. She was still able to make him forget his own best intentions.

He had gone there to apologize for seducing her, but as he watched her, Dane knew he wanted nothing so much as to touch her again.

Helen watched the smoldering cedar shavings darken from

the residual heat of the ashes, sensing Dane's desire without looking at him. She was astonished and irritated to discover that he still had the power to reach her without a word.

Damn you, Dane Corvin, she thought. Why? *Why?* And why *now?*

An odd answer came to Helen: Better now than at any other time in the last twenty years.

Josh is three thousand miles away, she thought. He is safe. You can settle this, once and for all, with Dane. You can tell him the rest of it, Waldo's part of it, and then send Dane away.

Calmer, Helen laid the two half-logs on either side of the smoking piece of cedar. After a few seconds, the kindling burst into flame from the heat of the underlying ashes. She watched while the small dancing flames lapped gently at the wood of the half-logs. A thin splinter of fuel caught, leaped, and the fire was reborn.

Like the fire inside her, except that this time the inner fire came from anger, not desire.

The room was silent for a while but for the gentle popping sound of the building fire.

"Your wood box is empty," Dane said quietly.

"I was just going to fill it when you showed up."

Helen rose from her knees and turned to face him.

Dane glanced through the window at the pile of log rounds in the side yard. "You have to split your own wood?"

"Josh split some before he left," she said quickly, seeming to defend the boy. "He promised to do the rest when he comes home at Thanksgiving."

"There isn't enough wood to last the week."

Anger suddenly flared in Helen's dark eyes. "I get along fine. I can cut my own wood, haul my own water, make my own way, so I'd appreciate it if you saved your comments about what my son did or didn't do."

"Sorry. I didn't mean to upset you."

"You haven't upset me," she shot back. "How I feel about you isn't new. It's pretty much the same as it was twenty years ago."

Dane looked away. Now there was anger in his eyes, too, although he tried to control it. For a moment, silence lay heavily between them. Then Helen drew a deep breath.

"You wanted to say something," she said. "So say it and then go. Whatever happened between us twenty years ago is long past. We both have lives of our own. We need to get on with them."

Dane stared at her, confused. He had sensed a softening in her when he talked about Dewey, but now she was cold and hard again. She still had the ability to surprise him, to keep him off balance, just as she had when they were both young. Now, though, she had a woman's power, the strength of life and experience. She was formidable, almost intimidating.

"I didn't come here to make you unhappy," Dane said. "Maybe I should have called ahead, except that I figured you wouldn't see me at all."

"You were right."

Dane shoved his hands into the hip pockets of his jeans in a gesture his coworkers had learned meant trouble. He spun and confronted Helen directly.

"Then I'm glad I walked in uninvited. This way, I get the chance to say something I tried to say twenty years ago."

"Don't bother. You couldn't have said anything that would have changed the outcome—then or now."

"I'm sorry, Helen. Damned sorry. That's what I wanted to say twenty years ago in the courthouse. That's what I've wanted to say to you for twenty years. What I did to you, lying that way, is the only thing I've ever done that I deeply regret."

Helen glared at Dane, saying nothing.

Dane shrugged. "You won't forgive me, and that's fine. What I did was unforgivable. But I wanted you to know how I felt."

"Is that really why you came? You don't know the rest of it?"

"The rest of what?" he asked, suddenly suspicious.

"Your apology would be nice for some folks, but it leaves me cold, and it means nothing at all to Waldo."

There was both warning and invitation in Helen's words. Dane sensed the trap and was silent for a moment. Finally, his curiosity won out.

"Okay. So what's wrong with Waldo now? Did he go on to bigger and better kinds of crime?"

Helen looked hard at Dane and felt some of her anger slipping away. He really didn't know.

"Waldo is dead," she said wearily.

She saw the shock in Dane's light green eyes, then the confusion changing his expression.

"When?" he asked.

"Fifteen years ago."

Dane's eyelids flinched. "What happened?"

"He died of an overdose in a dirty little alley off Pioneer Square in Seattle, a needle in his arm. He was a heroin addict. He picked up the habit in that federal prison where you sent him."

The moment Helen spoke, she felt the rest of the anger go out of her. It was replaced by a sadness deep enough to embrace her and Waldo and Dane, all at the same time.

"You've blamed me for that for twenty years?" Dane demanded.

Helen started to say something, then stopped. She thought for a moment, as though she had never questioned the source of her own rage.

"Yes, I guess I have," she said.

Dane removed his hands from his pockets and stared at them, as though to see whether they were stained with Waldo's blood.

They were not.

"Didn't Waldo have a part in it?" Dane asked coldly. "Lots of guys go to prison for a year and don't come out heroin addicts."

Anger leaped again, surprising Helen with its intensity.

"It wasn't the prison," she shot back. "It was the way you made Waldo feel before you put him there. He liked you, Dane. He liked you better than anyone else. Then you betrayed him. You hurt him bad, a hell of a lot worse than you ever hurt me. At least I got kissed on the way to being fucked."

Dane clenched his teeth. "I liked Waldo, too. That's why I went up to see him in the camp. I had an idea for getting him out early, finding him decent work, putting the pieces back together. . . ."

Abruptly, Dane stopped remembering, stopped feeling, stopped thinking about the irretrievable past. Only then did he trust himself to look at Helen.

"I can't believe I'm hearing this from you," Dane said. "Waldo didn't go to prison because I snuck up on him and pretended to be his friend. He went to prison because he was fishing illegally."

"But you—

"Waldo had no right to be angry," Dane interrupted. "He knew what he was doing, the risks he was running. You, now, you have the right to be angry. You didn't do anything. You were innocent."

"But I was—" Helen cut off her own words.

"Go ahead," Dane challenged her. "You were what?"

She took a deep breath and let it out, willing the anger to go with it.

"I was stronger than he was," Helen said simply. "Waldo was always so lonely. He didn't mind that, most of the time. That's why he was such a good fisherman. He could work by himself.

"Then you came along, and he found somebody who really seemed to understand. I think you were the only man he ever really wanted to be around, the only one he . . . "

Again, Helen was silenced by the truth she didn't want to speak.

Dane waited, his wolf's eyes alert, as though sensing that he finally had run his quarry to earth.

"Damn it," Helen said softly. "Damn *you*. You were always so smart, so quick, so understanding. Don't you see? Waldo loved you like a brother. Do you even know what love is? Do you have any idea what a lonely person will do for it?"

Dane looked from Helen to his hands. They had become fists. Slowly, he relaxed them.

"Yes," Dane said softly. "I do have some idea what a person will do for love."

His face was grim as he thought back over more than the past twenty years, seeing his whole lifetime and beyond, asking questions that had never had answers and never would.

He turned and stared out the side window into the yard. He looked at the pile of log rounds there for a long time.

"For what it's worth, I never worked undercover again," Dane said finally. "I stayed in the Fish and Wildlife Service, and I put a lot of guys in jail over the years, but I never lied to any of them. I took them straight up or I didn't take them at all."

Dane walked quietly to the door, opened it, and paused, looking out into the bright autumn day.

"I'm sorry that Waldo died," Dane said. "But I'm not nearly as sorry as I am that you're alive and still so full of anger."

"Waldo's death hasn't bothered me for a long time. Then you showed up and brought it all back."

"I came here to try and make things better, not worse," he said.

"Better for who? Yourself?"

Helen regretted the words the moment she said them, but the damage was already done. Hard, male anger flared up on Dane's face.

"To hell with it," he said. "This isn't doing either one of us any good. I'm out of here."

Dane hesitated for an instant, long enough to let Helen object, but she didn't. He went to the door, opened it, and walked out. He pulled the door shut hard behind him.

Helen felt a rush of grief as she watched Dane go. She started to cry out to him, thought of Josh, and set her teeth.

Trembling, she watched the window beside the door. After an instant, Dane walked past it. He stared straight ahead, his face still bleak with anger.

Helen turned and stared out the side window, watching for Dane to walk past the woodpile and out of her life. He moved slowly, looking around the yard as though trying to reorient himself.

Then Dane vanished.

Helen waited for the sound of a car. She heard only the harsh calling of a gull over the water. She felt like the gull's cry, empty and lonely and inhuman. The gull called again, then fell silent.

From the side of the house came the throaty laughter of a raven.

Tears burned against Helen's eyelids, astonishing her. Part of her cried out to her wolf, willing him to come back; but she was so rooted in her own uncertainty that she couldn't speak.

Then Helen heard a sharp, loud sound, puzzling yet familiar. She wiped away her tears and moved cautiously to the window, afraid to look and find only her own longings.

SIX

When Dane closed the cabin door behind him, he was shaking with emotion. Instead of resolution, he had found only increased regret. Instead of healing the past with words, he and Helen had reached a point where words were suddenly too dangerous to be used.

A seagull screamed, caught between sky and sea.

Dane drew a deep breath. The morning air tasted of salt from the bay in front of the house or from tears that had never been cried.

And would it have made any difference anyway?

Trying to understand what had happened in the past and what was still happening now, Dane stared out at the water. Waldo's death rankled. Even as a young man, Waldo had always been locked too tightly inside himself, set free only by a dozen beers at a time. For a man who drank like that, seeking oblivion, dope was the next step. Death was the last one.

Dane was not surprised that Waldo had taken both steps. Disappointed, but not surprised. He muttered a low curse that was also a prayer for Waldo and for Helen and for himself.

Then Dane headed for the road where he had left his truck. As he rounded the corner of the cabin, he stopped abruptly, staring at the ax Helen had buried in the chopping stump.

A lustrous black raven was perched on the end of the handle, watching him. The bird hopped on the slippery perch, then chuckled quietly, as though amused by the foolishness it had seen. A second raven, perched on the peak of the cabin's roof, echoed the softly mocking laughter.

Dane felt a twinge of uneasiness. These ravens seemed more magical—and more forceful—than the one on the roof of Dewey's house.

The raven hopped up and down on the ax handle again and made an odd, strangled noise. The noise came again, more clearly.

"Hello," the raven said.

The bird on the peak of the roof dipped its head eagerly, then responded, "Good-bye."

For a moment, Dane was dumbfounded.

The birds spoke again, repeating their strangled contradictions. Both of them watched him intently, as though they expected him to reply.

"Make up your minds," he retorted. "Hello or good-bye."

The ravens eyed him cannily and said nothing.

Dane chuckled at the irony of the moment.

The birds chuckled back.

Dane glanced around the side yard. His eye fell on the woodpile. Rounds of clean yellow Douglas fir, solid, sawed but not split, waited for the ax.

He remembered the empty wood box. Helen had put the last two split logs on the fire as he watched. They would chase the remains of the chill this morning, but the house would be cool again by evening.

Then where the hell would she be? Dane thought angrily. Fine young son Ted Hartel left with her. Josh doesn't even split the winter's wood for his mother. Typical teenager, I guess. He could use a little cold reality in his life. Obviously, Helen has spoiled him.

Like most middle-aged men, Dane had mixed feelings about the teenage male of his species. Most were full of themselves, thoughtless, energetic, and erratic. They wasted their energy and made a lot of noise, offending the world in the process, but they left so much undone.

And they created a lot of snarls for their adult selves to sort out later.

The second raven swooped off the roof of the cabin, sailed past his head, and settled on the roof of the small open-sided pole building that should have been filled with split firewood. The dark bird hopped down off the roof and settled on the handle of a splitting maul. It stared at Dane earnestly, then at the handle of the maul.

"I'll be damned," Dane said softly.

He walked toward the raven slowly, expecting it to take flight. The bird cackled excitedly but held its place. Finally, when Dane was a few feet away, the raven leaped into the air and circled around him, chuckling at its own cleverness in drawing man and maul together.

Dane picked up the maul and inspected it. The blade was tapered like an ax but weighted like a sledgehammer. The tool was well-used but still serviceable. He tested the heft of the handle as he moved to the tumbled pile of fir rounds.

With a smooth gesture that came of long practice, Dane shifted a round with the toe of his boot. Then he addressed the log, choked up on the handle of the maul, and swung it in an easy, overhead motion.

He brought the blade down in the center of the bright, clean log. There was a dry popping thud. The log fell neatly into two halves, split by the edge and weight of the maul.

The action seemed to delight the two ravens. They sprang into the air on long, strong wings and circled the woodpile, cawing and gronking to each other happily.

Dane grinned tightly, feeling an odd sense of release. He tipped one of the newly split half-rounds up on end and snapped the maul down into it almost casually.

The wood parted as neatly as if it had been cut by an invisible laser. The straight grain of the newly exposed wood was soft white gold.

Dane tipped the other half-round on end and split it. Then he kicked the new fireplace lengths to one side with his toe. He was positioning another full round when he sensed Helen at the corner of the cabin. He turned around, saw her staring at him as though he were some stranger, and turned back to the wood.

"What the hell do you think you are doing?" Helen asked.

Dane stripped off his vest and threw it over handle of the ax that was still buried in the kindling stump.

"You'll get cold long before Thanksgiving," he said.

"I'm fine. The wood's fine. I've chopped it most of my life."

Dane picked up the steel maul and inspected the number stamped into its side.

"You trying to tell me that you handle an eight-pound maul, Helen? You're strong but not that strong."

Helen brushed at the air with one hand, irritated that Dane should see through her so easily.

"Leave it alone," she said. "I can scrounge enough to last me until Thanksgiving, when Josh comes home."

"What makes you think Josh will have more time to chop wood during a four-day vacation than he had in the four months before he left for college?"

"Josh is a very responsible boy. He was just excited about going away to school. He didn't know how much would have to be done. . . ."

"So the firewood just got lost in the rush," Dane said.

Helen could hardly deny it.

Dane adjusted the new log with his toe, then stepped back and addressed it. He swung the maul easily in a full overhead arc, enjoying the flex and strength of his body. A split opened in the log, but large slivers of wood still held, joining the two halves. He grimaced, as though irritated at himself.

"I've been trying to split somebody's wood supply for a week now," Dane said, kicking through the splinters. "Dewey won't need his, but you will."

Helen shook her head even as she admired Dane's easy strength.

"I don't think it's such a good idea, Dane."

Dane looked at her. "It's just wood and it needs to be split. There's nothing complicated about it. If you don't want it for yourself, just figure that I'm doing your young Prince Josh a favor."

Helen felt her breath catch in her throat. She didn't reply for fear her voice might betray her. She crossed her arms in front of herself stiffly and looked past Dane.

When she kept her silence, he said, "I'll leave, if you really want."

She looked back at him, miserable and confused, and then at the log he had split so easily. Finally, she nodded a little.

"Go ahead, if you want," she said, her voice almost too low to be heard.

Dane bent over, turned up the two halves of the second log, and split each with a single, easy stroke. Then he moved on to the next log, kicked it upright, and cracked it with two blows. Quickly he fell into a measured workman's rhythm, focusing on the physical task and letting everything else slide away.

Helen watched silently, knowing she should leave but not able to force herself to do so. Slowly, she moved around to a place where she could see Dane's face, yet still stay out of the way of his maul.

The ravens cawed triumphantly and landed on the sloped roof of the open-sided wood crib. There they sat, watching the two humans with black, uncanny eyes.

"I see the birds have introduced themselves," Helen finally said.

"They pointed the wood out to me," Dane said, grunting a little as he sank the maul into a log whose grain was twisted and stubborn.

"They're Josh's. He's had them since he was twelve. They miss him. You're the first male they've seen around here since he left."

Dane nodded, filing that information. "Did he teach them to talk?"

"Oh, they greeted you, did they? I'm impressed. They usually only speak to Josh. He taught them. Not that 'hello' and 'good-bye' is a big vocabulary, but Josh is the only one I've ever seen who had the patience to teach ravens."

Helen's smile was warm and gentle as she thought about her son. The expression on her face stopped Dane in mid-swing.

"Something wrong?" she asked.

"That smile. You should bottle it and send it to Josh. He's probably lonely for it."

"I haven't smiled too much in the last couple of weeks," she admitted. "I miss Josh at least as much as Thought and Memory do."

"Thought and Memory?"

"The ravens."

Dane stared at the two sleek birds, amazed by their names. "Did you name them?"

"No. Josh did. The names are from Winomish mythology."

"Your boy doesn't sound like the average teenaged testosterone freak," Dane said slowly. "A Raven for a mother and talking ravens for pets. I'd like to meet Josh at Thanksgiving."

Quickly, Helen turned away to hide the expression on her face. She started back to the cabin.

"Where are you going?"

"I'm—" she stammered. "I'll get some gloves and help stack this."

Helen disappeared around the corner, leaving Dane confused all over again.

It took twenty minutes, but when Helen returned, her face was calm and composed. She had tied her hair back and pulled an old sweatshirt over her shirt. She handed Dane a pair of well-worn leather gloves before she pulled on a pair of her own.

By now, Dane had worked up a good sweat. His face was

bright and contented. He put aside the maul for a moment to pull on the gloves Helen had brought him. They fit. Surprised, he flexed his unusually long fingers. The gloves still didn't bind.

"Josh's?" Dane asked, holding up his hands.

Helen nodded.

"He must be a good-sized boy. His hands are as big as mine."

Helen looked away and regretted bringing out the gloves.

Dane swung his arms, twisting away tension in his shoulders. Then he bent over and began tossing splits of wood toward the crib where Helen would stack them. She picked up one of the splits and inspected it.

"You can still handle a maul," Helen said as she tossed the split in the direction of the crib.

"You sound surprised," Dane said, grunting a bit as he tossed a large section.

"Not really," she said, reaching for another piece of wood. "I just figured you'd be off in Washington or someplace, sitting behind a desk and giving orders instead of taking them."

"Nope. Matter of fact, I'm headed the other direction at the moment, geographically and careerwise."

Helen gave him a quizzical look.

Dane's shrug seemed stiff in a way that had nothing to do with the wood he had split.

"I've spent the last twenty years in the West and Northwest," Dane said. "I've had thirteen different duty assignments, from Montana to Colorado to the Ruby Mountains of Nevada, but always in the wide-open spaces. Now I'm headed for Alaska."

"Sounds good to me. You aren't happy?"

"It's a long story." Dane's tone said he would rather talk about something else.

"Okay. How about your family? All that moving must be hard on them."

"Don't have one, unless you count Dewey."

"Divorced?"

"Never married," Dane said without looking up. "I never settled down long enough."

"Since when does a man have to settle down to get married?"

Dane thought for a moment.

"I suppose a fisherman's wife might feel that way," he said, picking up a piece of split wood. "You must have had to raise the boy by yourself, even when your husband was alive. That's tough."

His back to Helen, Dane tossed the wood toward the crib. She straightened up and shifted her position, reaching for more chunks of wood.

"I knew what I was in for when I married Ted. He was a good husband, a good provider, a good father. Josh still worships the ground he walked on. He was a fine father, even though he wasn't here most of the time."

Helen's tone told Dane her family—past and present—was off limits for discussion. So many aspects of her life were closed to him that he wasn't sure what they could talk about comfortably.

"How about you?" he asked finally. "I was surprised to find you were still here. Judging from what I saw in the gallery, you're good enough to make it in the big time, and the paper said you've shown in some pretty fancy places."

"Shown in, but not lived in," Helen said.

"You don't like cities?"

"Not much. I'm not hungry enough, I guess. I tried Seattle for a little while, but it wasn't for me. A little like Mozart. Too many notes."

"So you live here by yourself, now that Josh is gone? You don't get bored?"

"Do you get bored, doing what you do, where you do it?"

He shook his head. "You couldn't pay me enough to make the city look good."

The split wood was piled in front of the crib, so Dane went back to work with the maul while Helen built parallel stacks of seasoned stove lengths. They worked in a companionable silence punctuated by the dry, hollow sounds of the maul striking wood.

The sun was high overhead and warm. Soon Dane stripped off his long-sleeved shirt and worked in his T-shirt. Without meaning to, Helen stopped to watch him for a moment. There was a solid, male thickness to Dane that seemed to come of natural conditioning and hard work, not hours in a gym.

As a man, Dane was still easy to take, intelligent and confident and calm. Only when Helen thought of him as the father of her child did she grow agitated.

After a time, Dane stopped and stretched, shaking his arms to settle the knotted muscles in his upper arms and shoulders. Helen looked around and realized that almost two hours had gone by. Dane had split more than a cord of the wood.

"That's enough," she said quickly. "I can't ask you to do any more."

"I'm fine. Straight wood, a good maul, a beautiful day. There's a bit of Zen in splitting wood, like willing the arrow into the center of the target. I needed that."

"Meditation?"

He nodded.

"Dewey's illness?" Helen guessed.

Dane hesitated and then nodded again. Dewey was half of Dane's dilemma. The other half was the woman stacking wood and watching him with eyes as dark and unreadable as a raven's.

"Our world hasn't figured out how to let a man die in peace," Dane said. "Sometimes it seems unwilling to let him live in peace, either."

Helen hesitated, unsure whether to pursue the intimacy implied by discussing problems.

"Would talking help?" she asked quietly.

Dane looked at Helen for the first time in the last hour. He let his glance touch her hair and roam slowly over her face.

"I don't know," he said. "I haven't had much talking in the last twenty years. I'll have to think a little about what to say."

"You think. I'll get us both some water."

Dane watched Helen walk back to the house. The sun caught

her dark hair, flecked now with a few touches of silver. Her back was straight and her head was high. She walked with the serene confidence of a mature woman and was more beautiful than he had ever remembered, now that the emotional storm between them had passed.

Helen returned a moment later with a large carafe of cool, fresh water and glasses. Dane drank deeply, nodded his thanks, and went back to work before the autumn air chilled him.

When the maul sank into wood once more, Helen set the water aside and sat down on a large madrone stump. After a moment, Dane began to talk as he worked, and Helen began to listen.

SEVEN

Dane's words came slowly, measured by the rhythm of the work. He talked about Dewey, about memories, and about the old man's pain and uncertainty.

"I guess dying isn't simple, even when you're ready," Dane concluded between steady swings of the maul.

"Learning to live is learning to let go," Helen said, thinking of Josh. "So is learning to die."

"Dewey would agree. He's letting go of things right and left."

Dane grimaced as he tried to break a log whose long fibers were twisted around an intruding branch.

"Is he frightened?" Helen asked.

"I don't think so. He just doesn't quite know how to go about doing what he has to do."

"Buddhists spend a whole lifetime learning that, and it still isn't easy."

Dane sank the maul into the stubborn log again. A crack opened, but twisted strands of wood fiber still held. He repositioned the log and struck it again. Still it held. Finally, he knelt beside it and levered it apart with his hands, ripping the last fibers.

"I guess that's why I like wood," he said, grinning savagely. "Unlike most of life's problems, wood will eventually yield to brute force."

Helen smiled. "I get the impression you're fighting something else, too, something that has little to do with your uncle."

Dane looked surprised. He stopped to stretch his left arm over his head, loosening muscles that had tightened. Then he began to tell Helen about the wolves and his choices.

When Dane was finished, they were both silent for a time. Helen picked at a curled, parchmentlike piece of red bark that had blown off a madrone tree beside the house.

"You said you're on your way to Alaska," Helen said quietly.

Dane nodded.

Helen didn't speak until she was certain her voice would be neutral.

"I'm a little surprised that you made that choice," she said.

Dane swung at a fresh round with such force that the log broke apart and the blade of the maul buried itself in the ground. He jerked the maul free and inspected the blade.

"I'll take the job," he said. "That doesn't mean I'll *do* the job."

Frowning, Helen looked at the man who was so like her son.

"What do you mean?" she asked.

"No wolf will ever be executed for murdering a caribou while I'm in charge of that program. But I'd appreciate it if you didn't say anything. The longer no one suspects, the longer the wolves will survive."

Helen felt a surge of relief. "I won't tell anyone."

Dane kicked the new stove lengths aside.

"I might kill a few of the old or the sick," he said, lifting the maul over a new piece of wood. "The wolves that would die anyway of disease or starvation. Predators aren't like prey animals. They don't have the luxury of a quick death.

"But as long as I can prevent it, nobody's going to be doing a body count of healthy wolves."

"Do your bosses know how you feel?"

"About wolves? They should. I've told them often enough."

"Then won't they be expecting you to drag your feet?"

Dane shrugged and slammed the maul into a fresh piece of wood.

"Of course they will," he said. "That's the whole reason for this game. They want me to fuck up. That way they can start the obligatory round of unsatisfactory ratings on my semiannual performance reports. In a year or two, they'll have enough black marks against me to retire me early or fire me outright."

Helen shook her head unhappily. "I knew bureaucrats and politicians could be vindictive. I didn't think they were smart, too."

"They just like to play God. But I've been around the government long enough to have learned all about obstructionism and obfuscation. They'll get me, sooner or later, but I'll make the bastards rue the day."

Dane smacked the maul into another log, hard. The blade hit at an odd angle and bounced sideways, pulling Dane off balance. He twisted awkwardly, trying to control the maul. When he straightened up, he grimaced.

"Are you okay?" Helen asked.

"No problem," Dane said, twisting and flexing his back. "I just got carried away. I should keep my mind on splitting wood. I've unloaded enough of my problems on you."

With that, Dane attacked another log.

Helen felt as though a door had been shut in her face. She wasn't used to male reticence. Josh was still too young, too dependent on her, to close her out.

But soon he wouldn't be. That was the whole idea of growing up.

Silently, Helen returned to stacking the logs. Soon, she caught up with Dane. When he kicked a new round into place for splitting, she spoke quickly.

"Hungry?" she asked.

Dane looked surprised, then nodded. "I could eat."

Helen laughed out loud at the typical male understatement. "Well, I'll see what I can find."

EVAN MAXWELL

"Don't go to any trouble."

"No trouble. I'll be right back."

Helen hadn't cooked for two since Josh left, but her pantry and freezer were still well-stocked. She pulled out two frozen loaves of homemade sourdough bread and a pot of homemade beef soup base. The soup went on a slow, low heat, and the bread went into the oven.

The frost had gotten the last of Helen's garden lettuce, but a few vine-ripened tomatoes had survived, along with carrots and red potatoes. All of them went into the soup. Twenty minutes later, with the soup cooking slowly, she went back to help Dane clean up.

Helen sensed immediately that something was wrong. Dane's shoulders seemed out of square. His work pace had slowed considerably, and he seemed to be favoring the left side of his body when he swung the maul. Unaware that she was back, he grimaced and stretched his arm up over his head, as though trying to ease a cramped muscle or a pinched nerve.

"Got yourself, didn't you?" Helen said knowingly. "I thought you had."

Dane turned around and started to deny the obvious truth. Then he shrugged and nodded.

"It spasmed up a little," he muttered, "once I started to cool off."

"Turn around. Let me see."

Instead of being level, Dane's left shoulder was higher than his right. With a skilled, impersonal touch, Helen traced the tightly bunched muscles that ran from his shoulder blade up to the base of his neck.

"There's a knot the size of a golf ball in this trapezius," Helen said.

"Thank you, Doctor Raven," Dane said with faint sarcasm.

Helen bore down a little on the cramp, and Dane twisted uncomfortably.

"You believe me now?" she asked.

"I believe you," he said through gritted teeth. "It happens all the time. I'll be all right."

"You'll be better if somebody works some of the lactic acid out of that knot out for you."

"Lactic acid? Since when did you become an expert on muscles and metabolism?"

"The Winomish have been studying the human body since long before some European dreamed up the word 'kinesthesiology.' My mother was one of the best natural practitioners my tribe produced this century. She taught me a lot. I picked up the rest over the years. Sometimes I think every bodywork discipline in the world has at least one devotee in the San Juans."

"A regular New Age hotbed," Dane observed skeptically.

"I've never quite figured out where New Age meets old," Helen replied. "My interest in bodywork is a bit more pragmatic. It was how I made my living before my art began to sell. So I'm not an expert, but I recognize trouble when I see it. Come on."

Dane grumbled uncertainly, like a big unhappy dog. Then he tossed the maul aside, picked up his shirt and vest, and followed Helen.

When he entered the house, Helen had already cleared off the waist-high table that had held her carving tools. She produced a thin pad from a drawer, spread it on the table, and gestured with her hand.

"Take off your T-shirt and lie down," she said.

Dane looked at the table.

"Uh, Helen, I'm fine, really. I don't need—"

"Will you please get on the table, sir. You won't be the first stranger who has been there. I've given about five thousand massages here in the last twenty years."

Helen examined Dane's body with a cool, clinical eye. "While you're at it, take off your jeans. Your lower back needs some work, too."

She pulled a flannel sheet from a nearby drawer.

"Since you're white-boy modest, I'll go in the other room. Just get on the table under this."

Helen handed Dane the soft sheet, turned, and disappeared into the kitchen.

Hesitantly, Dane stood in the sunlight from the west window. Finally he decided it wasn't the clinical intimacy, but rather the fact that he was expected to submit, that made him uneasy. However, his back did hurt, and he did recall Helen's magic touch.

So he stripped off his jeans, lay down on his stomach on the pad atop the table, and pulled the warm flannel sheet over him.

A few moments later, he heard the sounds of a microwave oven in the kitchen. Slowly, the aroma of warm, spicy food and baking bread penetrated his uneasiness.

"Ready, Doctor," he said dryly.

Helen emerged from the kitchen with a flannel-wrapped package and a heavy Turkish towel. She peeled the sheet from Dane's shoulder, rubbed something on his skin, and then laid the packet on his knotted trapezius muscle. Warmth spread across his back.

"Wow," he said. "Where'd you get that?"

"A combination of ancient and modern healing," Helen intoned. Then she snickered. "Actually, the rub is something called Tiger Balm. I get it at an Asian grocery in Seattle. The modern part is the hot water bottle. I nuked it in the microwave. Now lie still."

Helen laid the towel over the hot water bottle and rearranged the sheet so that the rest of Dane's back was bare. She spread her fingers across his lower ribs and rotated her hands, rubbing the skin against the bone beneath.

Almost instantly, Dane felt himself tense.

"Your muscles really are tied up," Helen said. "Try to relax. Sink into the table. Take a deep breath, let it out, and let your-self go."

Dane shifted his head until he could look out the window at

the afternoon light. He drew a deep breath and focused on the clean blue line of the far horizon. He took another breath and then another and let the rest of the world slide away.

Helen could feel the tension begin to dissolve in Dane's body. She worked silently for a while, bending and flexing her fingers over the first thin layers of tissue in his back, then stimulating the flat plates of muscles.

"You got lucky," she said finally. "I think you've just overdone it a little."

Dane grunted.

"It helps that you're in decent shape," Helen said, kneading his flesh impersonally. "Most men do nothing for six months or six years and then try to prove they've still got what it takes to split a cord of wood."

"Thanks for that professional appraisal. What are you doing, exactly?"

"Why? Am I being too hard on you?"

"No, but I'm beginning to feel like one of those Japanese beef cattle, the ones they massage every day so the meat stays tender."

Helen snickered. "The principle is the same."

Her fingers smoothed the first layers of muscles across Dane's shoulders and then went deeper. Each flat plate of muscle had its own knots. She scraped and straightened them one at a time until he shifted uneasily on the table.

"Hey," he grumbled, "I thought this was supposed to be a nice relaxing sort of thing."

Helen bore down with a little more force. "No pain, no gain. Isn't that how it goes?"

"Ow," he grunted. "Where did you hear that?"

"Josh, mostly. He ran cross-country for four years. He would get terrible cramps in his legs in the rain."

Helen drew the sheet back over Dane's shoulders, then rolled one corner of the sheet up off the lower part of his body and went to work on his calves and thighs.

As she worked, she felt her normal calm self-assurance begin to return. Once he lay down on the table, Dane was no longer the man who had been her lover, the man whose physical presence still unsettled her so. He became a human being whose body was in pain, out of adjustment.

Bodywork was something Helen understood. More important and intriguing, though, it was the first physical relationship with Dane that she controlled for herself. Her hands seemed to know the secret knots of his muscles intuitively. She loosened, straightened, and smoothed them, first with her thumbs, then with the points of her elbows.

Dane surrendered to the sensations that were neither pleasure nor pain, concentrating on the muscles as Helen worked them, trying to unbend the fibers with his own will. It was as though she was silently teaching him the muscular structure of his own back and legs.

For a time, the room was silent except for the sound of Dane's deep breaths and the faint ticking of the metal racks in the hot oven.

"You've learned a lot," Dane said, groaning. "Who was your professor, Himmler?"

"Oh, sorry," Helen said, easing off a bit. "Your calf is so strong, I didn't realize how deep I was going."

Dane let out a long sigh as he felt his leg relax from his ankle to his butt.

"Never mind," he said. "It was worth it."

Helen smiled and resumed working. Slowly, the massage became a kind of shared physical meditation, impersonal and yet intimate, relaxing because it was entirely without sexual content. The sun through the window was warm and a wave of contentment descended on Dane.

Helen drew the sheet down over Dane's legs and turned her attention back to his shoulder. The hot pack had transferred most of its warmth to his flesh. The knot in the muscle had dissolved, but the fibers were still sore. Helen worked them between her thumb and forefinger and then used her elbow.

"Let me know if it gets to be too much," she said.

Dane grunted and went back into his own mind, trusting her without realizing it.

Helen pushed down through the loosened muscles of Dane's shoulder, seeking the ligaments and tendons that bound his shoulder together. She found small trigger points in each bundle of tissue, pushing them as though they were switches, turning off the tension like an electrical current.

Her attention was so focused on the muscles beneath her hands that she forgot for a moment who or where she was. With gentle persistence, she carefully pushed Dane right to the edge of pain, then released the pressure and smoothed the newly straightened fibers.

"That's—" Dane muttered, preparing to object.

Helen moderated the pressure.

"—okay, right there," Dane finished. "Any more is too much of a good thing."

"Try to breathe around the pain," Helen advised softly, "or, better yet, *through* it. You've got some deep knots there. Feels like something has been gnawing at you. The wolves? Dewey?"

"Mortality," Dane said succinctly. "The wolves'. Dewey's. My own. You're lucky you've got a son. You know it doesn't end with you."

For a moment, Helen faltered. Then her hands resumed their unflinching work, seeking knotted muscles and kneading them until they were flat and supple.

Dane centered himself on the knots Helen had found and concentrated on his breathing. Slowly, he felt relaxation spread across the point of his shoulder and down his arms all the way to his fingers.

Helen sensed the change in Dane. Most people regarded massage as a passive process, but he was a quick study. He understood instinctively that he had to participate.

Finally, the long muscle fibers were aligned to Helen's satisfaction. She made a series of deliberate, slow passes across the muscles, then another series of sweeps down both sides of Dane's spine, using her elbow.

"That's the best anatomy lesson I ever had," Dane muttered. "Reminds me how everything is tied together."

"Yes, it is," Helen said.

Her voice was a little strained. Dane hadn't realized how much strength she was bringing to bear on him.

"You have a genius for this," he said, flexing his shoulder tentatively and then more deeply when he discovered that the muscles were free. "I'm not sure whether it's pain or pleasure, but I'm sure you're good at it."

"I was being very easy on you. If I had wanted to bear down, I could have crippled you."

"I don't doubt that a bit. But then who would split the rest of that wood?"

"Josh," Helen said firmly. "I want it waiting for him at Thanksgiving. Just a reminder, so he won't think he got away with something."

Dane felt a small rush of disappointment, as though Helen had suddenly cut the connection between the two of them. Splitting wood was a good excuse to hang around; he wasn't sure he would get a better one.

Helen grasped a handful of Dane's hair and tugged gently, scrubbing the muscles of his scalp against his skull. She did that several times, loosening his scalp. Then she released his hair, drew the sheet over him, and passed her hands across his shoulders lightly, signaling that she was through.

"There's a shower in the back bedroom," Helen said. "I'll toss you one of Josh's old T-shirts. By the time you're done, the food will be ready."

Dane finished a second bowl of the soup and half a loaf of hot sourdough bread before he slowed down. Finally, he scooped up a cube of red potato and inspected it with a critical eye.

"Fresh," he noted approvingly. "I don't seem to ever get enough of them."

"Bachelor cooking?" Helen asked. "Nuke something frozen and never say you're sorry?"

Smiling slightly, Dane shook his head. "I run a decent kitchen, if I do say so myself. But the way I've lived, I go for months in the field without fresh potatoes and vegetables. Meat is never a problem, but there are times I'd give a hundred dollars for a fresh tomato."

"You're a hunter, as well as a naturalist?"

"You eat what's at hand. Hell, I've probably eaten more endangered species than most people have *seen*. The difference being that out in the back of beyond, they aren't really endangered."

Helen laughed at his wry humor.

"Careful," Dane said, watching her. "A smile like that is a hell of a lot rarer than fresh vegetables in my life."

Helen felt her face flush. She discovered that she could not meet Dane's gaze. As long as he did not look at her, she was all right. Even while she was touching him, massaging the muscles of his back, she could control her response to him. But now, when she tried to look into the eyes that mirrored his soul, she flinched.

"Thank you for splitting wood," Helen said, moving her untouched food to one side. "I really do appreciate your help. The maul is not my weapon of choice."

Her tone was deliberately distant.

Dane stared at his plate for a long time, as though trying to make up his mind about something.

"Helen, I'd like to see you again," he said finally.

There it was, without preamble or explanation. But they both knew Dane's words were simpler than his meaning.

Helen looked down, hiding her eyes from Dane. She shook her head slowly, as though she had hoped this would not happen.

He sat waiting silently, but she didn't reply. Finally, he reached out carefully and touched the back of her right hand with his index finger.

She flinched and drew her hand back, as though his finger were a white-hot poker.

"This was a nice day," she said in a strained voice. "A better ending for us than the last one. Maybe we should just leave it that way."

Dane withdrew into his own space. "I would have settled for that when I arrived today. Not now. Now I want more."

His bluntness frightened Helen and made a shambles out of her attempt to withdraw. For an instant, she was tempted to tell him the truth about Josh. When Dane found out that she had deprived him of his own son, he would hate her as much as she had hated him when Waldo died.

Then Helen thought of the hunger in Dane's eyes when he looked at her for the first time in twenty years. His eyes said he wanted more, much more, than just to see her again. He wanted her, period. She was afraid she wanted him in the same way.

Helen felt as though she were floating away, losing control. She fought the sensation. It wasn't merely Dane's physical desire that intimidated her. Once, she had responded to that desire with her whole being.

But now he seemed to demand more of her than she felt able to give. It was a feeling that had little to do with Josh and a great deal to do with Helen herself. After years of struggle, she was finally getting her life back.

Now Dane came striding out of the past, watching her with his wolf's eyes, demanding that she share her life with him.

Helen sat frozen, caught between rational thought and sensual memory, between the twin ravens of hello and good-bye.

"I can't say yes," she finally whispered. "There's just too much . . . " Her voice trailed away helplessly.

Dane drew a deep breath. "At least you didn't say no, either."

Helen bowed her head. He was too quick. He had always been too quick.

For a time, Dane sat silently, seeking some ground as neutral as the woodpile had been.

"What you said this afternoon, about living and dying being a process of letting go," he said finally. "Do you think that's true?"

Helen glanced over, puzzled by the sudden shift in his thoughts. Then she nodded. "Why do you ask?"

"You helped me let go of a great deal of tension on the table this afternoon. Hell, you made me let go of so much, you damned near killed me outright."

He smiled gently, wisely leaving her space.

"But that got me to thinking. Dewey's in a lot of pain. He can't seem to relax. He's bound up tighter than a tick. Obviously, you understand these things. Can you think of anything that might help him?"

The question was so direct and unexpected that Helen blinked.

"I—" she stammered. "I could go see him, I suppose."

"I wouldn't ask that," Dane said quickly. "It's too much of an imposition. But if you had some idea that might help, I'd—"

"I don't mind," she interrupted as quickly as he had.

Dane hesitated and sighed, describing his reluctance without saying a word.

Helen met his gaze and nodded, assuring him.

"I've been in hospitals before," she said calmly. "I've seen people who are old, people who are dying. It's not an imposition."

That seemed to ease Dane. He smiled an off-center smile.

"Well," he said, "I'm damned sure Dewey would love a visit from a beautiful woman."

Helen smiled. It had been years since anyone had complimented her in that way.

"I'll be glad to see Dewey."

Dane waited and hoped that she would say more.

"As for the rest, I'll have to think about it," Helen said. "I'll have to think hard."

EIGHT

Dewey had been moved into a private room at the nursing home. He called the place "a sally port to hell." Dane understood what Dewey meant. Both of them were waiting, although for different outcomes.

The two men sat together for three days, talking, watching television, even playing gin when Dewey was able to concentrate. He seemed grateful to have been spared the exploratory surgery. He didn't mention death, or the future.

Some of the time, Dewey was lucid, even alert. The rest of the time, he was subdued and withdrawn because of the pain, the medication, or both.

Dane allowed Dewey to set the course and pace of their conversations. Most of the time, serious subjects were avoided. Dewey could watch the images on the tube, but his eyes were too bad to make out print, so Dane read scraps and snippets from local papers, fishing reports or science news or local gossip.

Dewey's mind had always been active and interested in the world around him, well-versed in science and the arts. But as the days passed, Dane sensed a slow downward spiral in his uncle's attention. At times, the process seemed purposeful, almost as though Dewey was slowly and deliberately snapping the fragile strands that still tied him to life.

Even though it was difficult to watch, Dane did nothing to discourage the process. He felt that Dewey had made a choice and was prepared both to live and to die with it.

The subject of Helen didn't arise until the third day. Dewey had been unusually clear and connected for a while, riding the bubble of pain medication before it broke and sucked him into the half-world of drugs. He sat up in the bed, propped against some pillows, staring at some talking heads on CNN.

"Foolishness," he exclaimed suddenly. "More damned foolishness that doesn't mean a thing." He stabbed his finger at the remote control, muting the arguing heads. "Let's talk about something important. Did you go out and see that woman?"

Dane was caught unprepared. He nodded.

"Well, what happened?" Dewey demanded.

His eyes were bright, as though he were a little drunk with pain or morphine.

Dane searched for some relatively neutral description of his meeting with Helen.

"We talked," Dane said. "There was some old business to sort out. Her brother and I had been friends. He's dead now, and Helen's still pretty broken up about it."

Dewey waited impatiently.

"I split some wood for her," Dane added reluctantly. "It seems her boy had forgotten to do his chores before he left. She fed me a meal . . . and that's it."

"For the moment," Dewey added.

Dane made an ambiguous gesture that could have been agreement or a reluctance to argue.

"Actually, she might drop by to see you sometime," Dane said.

"Me? What in hell for?"

"I told her about your shoulder. I twisted mine splitting wood. It tied up in a stitch like the one you always complain about. She has studied massage, and she managed to straighten me out. I thought she might be able to give you some relief, too."

Dewey extended his thin arm and tried to flex his shoulder.

"Medicine like that would be fine, if it worked," he said. "A damned sight better than any of these drugs they're pumping into me, even though it's too late."

Through the half-open door to the room, Dane caught a glimpse of Helen in the hallway. She was wearing a dark green sweater and a loose cotton skirt. Her hair was pulled back and tied with a green bow. The color made her look dark and strong.

"Hi," she said tentatively. "Maybe this is a bad time?"

Dane got to his feet quickly and went to the door.

"No, no, come on in," he said. "We were just talking about you."

Helen came in warily, as though she wasn't sure whether she should be there. She carried a bundle wrapped in newspaper. Dane glanced at it curiously.

"I'm sorry I didn't call ahead," she said to Dane, "but I wasn't sure whether I'd be able to get by. Then I found these this morning."

Helen pulled back the paper wrapping and revealed an armload of fall flowers. She turned quickly toward Dewey, who was trying to sit up on the bed to greet her.

"Please don't bother, Mr. Corvin," she said. "I'm Helen Hartel. You taught my son, Josh, when you were a substitute in honors biology last year. Josh still remembers you. He mentioned your lecture on evolution last night when I talked to him on the phone."

Dewey let himself slowly back down onto the pillows, then reached out a frail, cool hand to Helen.

"I remember Josh," Dewey said. "Every teacher in the system does. He's a fine young man."

Dane was startled. Before this moment, Dewey had never mentioned knowing Josh.

"Dane said the other day that you had missed the best part of autumn while you were in the hospital," Helen said, laying the paper bundle in Dewey's lap, "so I brought a little of it to you."

Dewey peeled back the paper with care. Helen had arranged a giant burst of solid and multicolored dahlias and chrysanthemums against a spray of maple leaves that had been frosted to a pleasing autumn red.

"Well, well, well, will you look at that," Dewey said softly, staring at the red and orange and yellow flowers with an almost childlike wonder. He brushed his quaking finger across a few bright petals. "Thought I might not get to see another dahlia that pretty."

Then he reached out impulsively with his right hand. Helen caught the gnarled fingers between her palms and let him hold on to her.

"That's quite a bunch of flowers, Mrs. Hartel. Thank you very much for bringing them."

For a moment, Dane felt a bit chastened that he had not thought of bringing some flowers himself. Then he studied the arrangement and realized his own efforts would not have had the same effect. Helen had a sense of color that was daring, but it worked magnificently.

Dewey looked up from the arrangement, searching the room for something and not finding it.

"I need a vase or something for this." Dewey turned to Helen. "That's the problem with these places. A man doesn't have his own stuff anymore. I've got the perfect vase for this, but it's standing on a shelf at home."

Helen stroked Dewey's hand gently. "Losing your favorite things is hard."

Dewey looked into Helen's dark eyes, sighed, and left his hand between hers. He began talking about dahlia varieties and colors. She listened, stroking his hand, and added the names and colors of her own favorite dahlias.

Dane felt as though he were invisible. He started to speak, thought better of it, and left the room to look for a vase.

Five minutes later, he was back with a plain glass jar the head nurse had grudgingly produced from a storeroom. Helen was seated on the edge of Dewey's bed, still holding his hand, and talking to him about the nature of his pain with the same candor and ease with which she had talked about flowers.

Dane took the flowers and arranged them inexpertly in the vase. Then he settled into a corner of the room and watched.

Helen's empathy was remarkable. So was her honesty. Asking the kinds of plain, simple questions that a good doctor would have, she drew Dewey into a discussion of his deteriorating condition and his feelings about it.

Dane realized as he watched that he and Dewey had been avoiding the subject. He also began to suspect that Dewey desperately needed to discuss death openly.

As the old man talked, he flexed his free hand unconsciously, drawing it into a fist and then extending the bony fingers as though he were reaching for something.

Helen asked a quiet question about pain in that hand. As she did, she released the hand she had been holding and gently captured the other, painful hand. Without looking at it, she began to gently, firmly trace its contours.

"Does this hurt?" Helen asked, pressing the ball of her thumb into the center of his palm.

Dewey shook his head, then nodded. "I guess it is a little sore."

Deftly, Helen ran her fingers over his hand and wrist and up his arm. She closed her eyes as she worked, as though that helped her to visualize the flesh beneath Dewey's skin.

She explored the wasted muscles and the stiff ligaments that attached them to brittle bone, but her touch was so gentle that the dying man evinced no pain. When she reached the point of his shoulder, she stood up and explored the joint carefully.

Dewey's white eyebrows suddenly jerked up his forehead.

"Painful?" she asked.

He nodded.

"I thought so," she said. "There are some spasmed muscles resting right on the bone. Would you let me work on them?"

Dewey nodded sheepishly, like an eight-year-old who was too bashful to ask a favor.

Dane had seen that expression often in the past few days, and each time he had been surprised by it. It was as though a ghost child lived beneath the eroding surface of the adult, waiting to show itself at odd moments.

Senescence seemed a constant battle between mature reason and doddering childishness. The outcome was inevitable; the ghost child would win. But strong-willed people like Dewey were often able to delay the outcome.

Helen gave Dane a quick glance that seemed to ask for help. Yet when Dane moved toward the bed, Dewey suddenly stiffened and began to resist the relaxation that had spread through his body. Clearly, he was willing to reveal weakness and pain to Helen but not to Dane.

Dane moved away, into the background again.

With gentle care, Helen helped Dewey out of his shirt. The old man's body was shocking in its boniness. Dewey was wasting away with each shallow breath he took.

Groaning slightly, Dewey rolled to one side and let Helen position him on the bed. Slowly, she went to work on the thin tissues of his back and shoulder, loosening the superficial layers and then reaching down through them, almost as though she were reaching inside the old man's skin to straighten ligaments and tendons.

After a moment, Dewey sighed. Dane could see one side of the bony old body relax and sag.

"Too much?" Helen asked gently.

"No, no," Dewey said quickly. "I don't know what button you pushed, but it's a hell of a lot more effective than morphine."

They talked quietly, Helen explaining to Dewey what she was doing and why, Dewey asking occasional questions. She talked about breathing, as she had with Dane. She encouraged Dewey to breathe through the pain and to visualize the muscles and tissues that were transmitting the bitter poisons to his nerves.

"There are an awful lot of them," Dewey mumbled.

"I know it's hard," she said, "but it really does work. I've used the method myself."

"What does a young woman like you know about pain?"

"Did you ever hear of childbirth?" she asked.

Dewey made a soft, rustling noise, an old man's laughter.

When Helen's head turned slightly in Dane's direction, he felt a stab of alarm. Her eyes were glazed, unseeing. She was focused completely on the knots in Dewey's body. Dane could see that physical contact with pain was costly to her.

He shifted in protest, moving to her aid. Her eyes focused on him, understood, and refused. She gave him a quick shake of the head and a wan, reassuring smile.

Reluctantly, Dane accepted that there was nothing for him to do at the moment. This was a meditation for two. Helen was compassionate enough to accept the cost.

Dane eased out of the room and pulled the door closed quietly behind him. He stood in the gloomy institutional hallway for a moment alone. Then the tears welled up in his eyes and rolled freely down his cheeks.

NINE

An hour later, Helen pulled the door of Dewey's room closed behind her and leaned against it for a moment. Her legs were suddenly wobbly. She had not given so much of herself in a long time.

She had left Dewey in a deep, natural sleep. He was relaxed and breathing evenly, the grip of his pain broken for the moment. Helen knew the pain would return and so did the old man, but for the moment, there was peace.

A nurse came down the hall carrying a stainless-steel tray covered with a crisp linen towel.

"Are you all right, ma'am?" she asked Helen.

The nurse was cool and starched and calm, the sort of woman who could manage life and death for eight hours a day and then go out to an aerobics class.

"I'm fine," Helen said quickly. "Is that for Mr. Corvin?"

The nurse nodded and checked her watch. "His pain medication is already half an hour late." Her tone conveyed disapproval.

"Do you suppose you could hold off awhile? He just got to sleep."

"Without his shot? That's not likely. His pain has been acute."

"I spent the last hour working with him," Helen said. "His pain was mostly from muscle spasms in his back and shoulders. I managed to break down most of them."

The nurse suddenly looked suspicious. "Are you some kind of massage therapist?"

Helen straightened up but continued to block the door. She was used to medical disdain.

"No," Helen lied, "I'm a member of the family, and I want that medication withheld until Mr. Corvin lets you know that he needs it again. He's fully capable of making that decision himself."

"But his doctor said—"

"If there are any questions," Helen interrupted, "you can confirm my order with his nephew, who has power of attorney for health care."

Then Helen stood her ground in front of the door until the nurse finally turned and stalked down the hall on soundless rubber soles.

With a small smile of triumph, Helen went to look for Dane. She found him sitting in the warm sun on a side lawn. He was composed now, but she could tell that he had finally confronted his own emotions and his own reality in Dewey's withered body.

Mortality, the curse and the blessing of human existence.

Helen had confronted more than her share of deaths. She knew what it was to accept the imminent and unavoidable loss of someone she loved.

But she had seen something else in Dane's eyes, the moment before he left Dewey's room. Dane's unhappiness went beyond the dying of a favorite uncle.

Dane believed he was losing his last blood relation. Unlike many people, Dane could take no comfort from a family continuity that transcended death, Corvin grandfathers and fathers and grandchildren, Corvin uncles and nephews and grand-nephews, each generation of Corvins supplanting the other and being supplanted in turn.

The only comfort for the hospice was the nursery, the intimate, unbroken connection of family lines.

And Helen had deprived Dane of that comfort with her

choices and her half-truths. Dane's sense of family died with Dewey Corvin. The Corvin family line died with Dane.

Helen stopped short, suddenly light-headed again.

Dane looked up to see Helen standing on the sidewalk, ghostly pale in the sunlight of late afternoon. He came to his feet quickly and moved toward her. She seemed to waver. He caught her and held her against him.

At first, Helen was stiff. Then she leaned against Dane's strength, accepting his support and aching to end his pain. She could tell him about Josh, but at what a terrible cost to her son. And to herself. She might have earned that anguish, but had her son?

Helen opened her mouth and tried to speak, but all that came out was Dane's name.

"Easy, easy, easy," he whispered.

Dane felt her body against his, soft and yielding. Then he felt her shoulders grow stiff, as though she was trying to back away.

"Relax," Dane said gently. "I'm sorry I asked you to work with Dewey. I had no idea it would cost you so much."

Helen hid her face against Dane's shoulder. For the first time in twenty years, she understood what his own lie must have cost him, that night when they lay together in the forest.

For the first time in twenty years, she came close to forgiving him.

But she could not speak about the child they had conceived. Josh still came first, and the truth would destroy his childhood and his emerging, still-fragile identity as an adult.

She had spent twenty years making certain that Josh wouldn't pay for her mistake. The truth would cut the ground from beneath Josh's feet.

Helen allowed herself the luxury of ten more seconds inside the circle of Dane's strong arms. Then she shifted subtly and stepped back.

"Dewey's asleep," she said. "I hope you don't mind, but I told the nurse I was a member of the family. She wanted to give him a pain shot. I told her to leave him alone."

Dane threw his head back and laughed, surprising both of them.

"I don't mind," he said, "and I'm sure Dewey will get a bang out of it. He hasn't had much to smile about this week. But since you're now an honorary Corvin, come on, I've got something to show you."

Dane turned toward the parking lot and tried to turn Helen at the same time. She resisted the pressure of his hand.

"I've got to get going," she said. "There's a ferry back to Raven in twenty minutes."

"There's a ferry every hour," Dane said gently. "I have something that I want to show you. It won't take long."

Helen gave in, but she didn't speak again until they were in his truck, headed out of town along the narrow Langley Highway.

"Where are we going?" she asked.

"About four miles down the road," Dane said, smiling to himself. "I need some advice and you're the perfect choice. In return, I'll fix you a cup of coffee. Maybe one with a shot of brandy. You look like you could use one."

The idea was intoxicating by itself. Helen could almost feel the brandy's warmth spread through her. She lay back against the headrest and looked out through the trees to the water. The highway ran across a clearing, giving a view of the dark green islands beyond. She let the landscape seep through her tightly held emotions.

Dane turned the truck down a neatly graveled road that led toward a wooded point overlooking the strait. He drove with an anticipatory grin on his face, enjoying his little surprise.

The land on either side of the gravel road was recovering from a thirty-year-old clearcut. Alder and willow were mixed with second-growth Douglas fir and cedar. Then the truck rounded a bend and suddenly they were back in an old-growth forest.

Helen felt the gentle strength of the old trees wash over her like a benediction. Without realizing it, she sighed.

Dane pulled up beside a neat old garage, got out, and held Helen's door for her. She looked at the hundred-foot firs above and around her and listened to the sound of the wind in their tops.

"Dewey's?" she asked.

Dane nodded. "He wanted me to have it before he dies. The house is the wife Dewey never had, and the kids, and the grand-kids. Now the house is mine . . . "

Helen looked away from Dane, unable to bear the pain that came from his words.

"Come look," Dane said.

He took her elbow and guided her gently to the head of the broad cement stairway that led down the steep slope from the garage to the house.

Helen took in the long, gracefully designed stairs, the sturdy, stout house with its gray-weathered cedar shake siding and the view of the water beyond. Her artist's eye caught a thousand small touches—the stained glass brow windows that glinted in the late light, the carefully tended rhododendrons and azaleas that blended with the natural salal and fireweed, the wind-sculpted firs that surrounded and framed the views. Each part was thought out and plainly executed, but the entire impact was smooth and seamless.

"I understand Dewey better now," Helen said softly. "His house is unique."

"Yes. It's a shame his straightforward view of life won't be passed on."

"He has you."

Dane nodded and said nothing.

After a moment, he continued down the stairs, drawing Helen with him. She looked through the sweeping limbs of the trees to the ocean beyond. Raven Island lay across the strait, only eight miles away.

How eerie, she thought. This house that Dane and Dewey built has been here for twenty years, and I never knew it.

Then, unhappily, came another thought. Josh would love the house overlooking the sea and the islands of his childhood.

The big front door was a masterpiece of hand-crafted oak and cherrywood. Dane slid the latch open and stood back so Helen could enter.

She hesitated, uncertain. The afternoon had drained her, leaving her weak and vulnerable. She wasn't sure she ought to be in the same room with Dane. There was something even more unsettling about being alone with him in a house that had been Dewey's and now was Dane's.

"It's important to me," Dane said, seeming to sense Helen's uneasiness. "I think it will do you good, too."

Helen drew a deep breath and stepped over the threshold into a foyer furnished with beveled-glass mirrors and an antique secretary that reached almost to the ceiling. Her eyes were still adjusting to the interior light when Dane led her into the living room.

Helen stopped and simply stared. The entire west wall of the house was glass. The house was filled to overflowing with the glow of the late-afternoon sun.

Slowly, Helen looked around, admiring the open, airy design of the interior. The rooms of the second floor were arranged in a horseshoe shape, leaving a beautiful central space with a vaulted ceiling that arched more than twenty feet above the main floor.

Then Helen felt an odd sensation, almost as though she were being watched by someone—or something—other than Dane. She looked around the interior with a quizzical expression.

Dane grinned and took Helen gently by the shoulders. He turned her toward the back wall of the large cathedral-like room.

"Some old friends have come to live with me," he said.

An elegant raven totem stood blackly against the dark red branch of a stylized cedar tree. The raven was staring down on the humans with dark, clear eyes that had seen all of man's folly. Behind the thick base of the cedar, concealed except for half of his head, the wolf watched them almost playfully through a dangerous green-gold eye.

Helen felt a surge of joy. Her most difficult work had found its natural home. The wall and the house made a perfect setting for a piece of art that had been impossible to place, until Dane had come and seen and understood how to match the strength of the art with the strength of the house.

"Oh, Lord," Helen said softly. "What have you done, Dane? What have you done?"

She stared up at the *Wolf and Raven* for a long time. The art fit the space like a miracle, transforming everything, even itself. She would never again be able to imagine either of them alone.

Dane took a step and stood so close behind Helen that he caught the clean scent of her hair. He could tell the instant she sensed his presence. Suddenly she was poised like a half-wild raven, shy and unpredictable. He desperately wanted to touch her, but he didn't want to risk making her flee.

"I thought your art fit very, very well, but I wanted your opinion," Dane said.

Helen looked over her shoulder at him, shaken by emotions that she could not put into words. Finally, she looked away from the living wolf to the memory and dream she had carved.

"I don't think there's another wall in the world that can stand up to it," she said simply. "Thank you."

"It's the artist who deserves the thanks."

Dane closed his hands around Helen's shoulders and squeezed gently. He released her more quickly than he wanted to and moved away into the kitchen.

"Coffee, brandy, or both?" he called out.

Helen stared at the raven and the wolf for a long time before she spoke.

"It had better be coffee," she said. Then she added too softly for Dane to hear, "There are enough spirits around as it is."

An hour later, Dane and Helen sat in rocking chairs facing each other. The chairs were positioned so Helen could watch the sunset light change the wolf and the raven on the wall. The setting sun softened the faint lines around her eyes and deepened the warm tone of her skin.

"Aren't they going to get lonesome, if you go off to Alaska this winter?"

Dane smiled into his coffee cup. "There's still a little bit of room up there. Maybe you could find them a friend or two."

Helen studied the cedar carving, then the rest of the house.

"You and Dewey built this whole place yourself?" she asked.

Dane nodded. "I worked on the framing the summer after I got out of school and the following summer, the one we met. Dewey did most of the finishing over the last twenty years, one job at a time.

"He sort of ran out of time, though. Not everything got done. The floors in this room were still a little rough. I sanded them down and refinished them."

Helen traced the whorls of grain in the red oak floor with her eyes. She loved soft woods, fir and cedar, but the cinnamon-colored patterns of the hardwood grain gave the floor a life of its own, as though the spirits of the living trees had somehow been preserved in the finished lumber.

"Some people think we shouldn't cut a single tree," she said, "but this kind of careful work makes you understand that carpentry can be an act of devotion."

"Dewey always thought of it that way, though he rarely talked about it."

"Did he always live here alone?"

Dane nodded, then stared out at the setting sun.

"He fell in love once. She sent him away," Dane said quietly. "I guess he didn't think he could bear the pain enough to take another chance."

They both were silent for a time.

"How about you, Dane? I'm surprised you never had a family."

He shrugged carefully.

"I'm a little surprised myself," he admitted. "I was . . ."

Dane searched for the right words, words that wouldn't send Helen flying from the house like a startled raven.

"I didn't really feel like settling down after I left here," he said finally. "I moved around a lot on the job."

"No serious relationships?" Helen asked before she could stop herself.

"A couple."

Dane stared out the window for several seconds more than he should have. When he looked back at Helen, his eyes seemed troubled by a memory.

"Only one, actually," he said.

Helen sensed that the memory of that relationship had been in his thoughts as he sat in the sunlight and cried over Dewey.

"What happened?" she said, pressing gently.

Dane looked a little surprised at her persistence. Then another emotion slipped past his guard. It might have been anger. She couldn't tell.

"We had a disagreement over family," Dane said, biting off each word. His eyes were savage. "She didn't want one. We were together for a year. Then I found out that she had gotten pregnant and had an abortion without talking to me."

He turned and looked at Helen with a mixture of rage and restraint.

"Call it old-fashioned," Dane said, "but I believe the father ought to have a say. It's his life, too."

Helen's throat ached with half-truths that added up to a single unforgivable lie, but she forced herself not to look away from the father of her son.

"So you broke up?" she asked.

"I walked out. I didn't trust myself to get within arm's reach of her again. Ever. It's the only time in my life I wanted to hit a woman. When I think of what she took away from me, I—"

Abruptly, Dane stood up and walked to the kitchen, radiating a rage and pain that hadn't dimmed through the years.

Helen understood how he felt. She had spent too much time feeling that way herself.

Silently, she watched the setting sun. The autumn light was

soft and gentle, but her eyes burned as though she were gazing at a noon sky. Silent tears coursed down her cheeks.

Love is dangerous, Helen thought. It is the most treacherous emotion in the world.

Evening darkness had descended over the sea and the distant islands when Helen came out of her own thoughts and realized that she was still alone. She had sat in the cherrywood rocker, wrestling with her own demons, for what seemed like only moments, but the sky told her more than an hour had passed.

Noises came from the kitchen. Not angry noises as before, but the restful sounds of pans and a faucet being turned on and off. Finally, she smelled food.

A meal, nearly complete. It was too late to object, too late to flee.

She had been right, love was both dangerous and treacherous. It was also more powerful than she had remembered.

TEN

Dane cooked as he lived, with both flair and precision. There was a pot of sauce made from Dewey's home-canned tomatoes on one burner and a sizzling pan of local sausages on the other. He had washed some romaine lettuce from the garden and was tearing up the crisp leaves for a salad.

When he saw Helen in the doorway, he turned up the burner under a steaming pot of water. It boiled immediately and vigorously. He dropped in a handful of angel hair pasta.

"You sleep as deeply as you work," Dane said. "Feeling better?"

"Sleep? I guess maybe I was. I'm sorry."

"Why? Dinner is almost ready. You want a glass of wine?"

Dane nodded to an open bottle of Washington merlot and two glasses, one of which was half-full.

"I think I'd better stick to coffee," Helen said, walking to the counter where an electric percolator stood.

Dane picked a fresh cup off a shelf and poured it full. Then he went back to the food. He speared the cooked sausages out of the pan, sliced them on a cutting board, and then swept them into the sauce with an unconscious flourish.

"Did you take lessons to learn that?" Helen asked. "You're very impressive."

"Cooking for one is boring unless you make a show of it," he said. "How are you at grating Romano?"

They spoke little after that. The preparation and the eating of food kept them involved. Helen thought she wasn't hungry, until Dane produced a fresh loaf of bread from the oven. Its aroma and the rich homey smells of the rest of the dinner made her suddenly famished. As she ate, she felt her energy return.

Then Helen surprised herself by accepting a glass of wine. The merlot's soft, round warmth spread through her. Dane refilled her glass, and she didn't object, although a small warning bell sounded in the back of her mind.

They finished eating, having talked quietly of nothing in particular, and Dane put on a pot of fresh coffee.

"The evenings are a little chilly," he said. "Why don't you build a fire in the fireplace while I clear up?"

The alarm sounded in Helen's mind again, louder this time.

"I really should be going. The last ferry is at nine."

"That's why I'm making coffee," Dane said. "But I still need the fire. Dewey's heating bills would be killers without one."

Helen took the glass of wine with her into the living room and set it resolutely on the mantel, out of reach. She felt light-headed enough around Dane without adding to the problem.

She quickly laid a fire and kindled it with smoothly split cedar. Then she sat on the couch, watching the light of the flames play on the wall and the carving she had made so many years ago. The flickering firelight added mystery to the piece. She could almost hear the bird and the wolf talking quietly to each other, kindred spirits sharing different bodies.

In a few minutes Dane brought two cups of fresh, fragrant coffee on a tray and set it on the old oaken table in front of the couch. He sat down beside her and sweetened the coffee in his mug, stirring a precise half-teaspoon of sugar with three twists of his wrist, then putting the silver spoon aside and tasting the result.

The coffee brought a mellow, contented smile to his face. He took another sip, then set the mug down and looked at her.

Helen watched the small ritual with a mixture of emotions. There was an intimacy to it that was magnetic. She could feel the warmth of Dane's leg a few inches away from hers on the couch. The unfinished glass of wine sat on the mantel, but the glow of the meal and the previous glass still lingered within her.

Dane shifted and settled back into the couch. His shoulder brushed against hers.

Helen was on her feet almost before she realized it. She marched to the mantel to retrieve the glass of wine, using it as an excuse for leaping to her feet without warning. Automatically, she took a gulp of wine.

Dane watched Helen move away with an odd, still smile on his face. He waited another moment, then slowly got up and followed her.

Helen turned away as he approached, facing the fireplace as though inspecting the fire she had built.

"You sure you want more of that wine?" Dane said. "I thought you were worried about driving, a minute ago."

Helen glanced at the glass in her hand.

"Yes," she said, taking another gulp. "I mean, no."

She set the glass down again and tried to think of something to say that would make Dane move away from her.

Dane stood silently for a moment, a foot behind Helen, studying her hair and her neck and the curve of her shoulder. Then he reached out and rested his left hand on her left shoulder, at almost the same spot she had first touched him when he was splitting wood on Raven Island.

"You're as tight as a tick, and I don't mean the wine," he said softly. "You really ought to do something about those spasms in your trapezius."

The words, like the touch, were a mirror image of what Helen had done and said to Dane. She shivered faintly at his warmth. She tried to quell the tremor. She knew that he could feel it in her body.

"Dane, don't."

She breathed the words so softly she wasn't sure he could hear them.

"I'm not trained," Dane said gently. "I don't have your touch. But somebody's got to treat the doctor, too, don't they?"

His long, strong fingers curled over the spot of tension that burned at the base of Helen's neck. First with one hand, then with both, he traced the lines of her shoulders. All the muscles were tight, too tight. He rested the tips of his fingers on the points of her collarbone. Slowly, he probed with his thumbs, seeking the individual bands of muscle and the spots where muscle attached to bone, mimicking the touch she had used on him.

"It's not as easy as you make it seem," he said after a few moments. "What's the secret?"

"The secret?" Helen said distractedly. "I . . . you . . . "

Sighing, she surrendered to the sensation of Dane's hands on her body and gave up trying to finish the sentence.

Dane closed his eyes as he tried to visualize the complex network of muscle and tendon and ligament beneath his fingers. He had studied anatomy. He knew what the structures should look like. But he couldn't find the right combination of pressure and motion.

And his mind kept wandering as he worked.

After a moment, he lightened the pressure. Helen immediately seemed to relax a little. Her shoulders sagged. She drew a deeper breath.

"That's better," she said quickly, seemingly relieved that he had stopped.

"I could still bounce nickels off you," Dane said, pushing into a tight mass of muscle halfway between her neck and the point of her shoulder. "You're not helping me at all. Stay right there for a minute."

Dane moved away and Helen allowed herself to relax. She felt light-headed again, but she could no longer blame the wine. She reached out blindly for support. Her hand brushed the cool rock of the fireplace. She leaned against it and drew deep breaths. She thought of Josh, her talisman, her grounding. If she could keep him in her mind, she might be able to withstand Dane's gentle, relentless campaign for her.

Dane came back carrying a thick roll of leather. He undid the strap that contained the roll and laid out a deep white sheepskin rug on the hearth. When he was finished, he gestured toward the rug.

"You can't get a good massage standing at attention," he said. "Even I know that."

Helen stared at the deep, soft pelt. Slowly, she shook her head.

"No, Dane, I don't think so . . . "

"You can dish it out but you can't take it, huh?"

She straightened her shoulders. "I'm fine, really. I have to be going."

Dane put his hands on Helen's shoulders and shook his head. "It's all I can do to repay you for all you've done for me."

Then he kissed her lightly on the corner of the mouth.

The pressure of his lips was so unexpected that Helen almost gasped. She stared at Dane, speechless, as though she had received an electrical shock instead of a kiss.

Gently, Dane guided Helen down to the pelt. He made her stretch out on her stomach. Then he dropped to his knees, positioned himself at her head, and went to work on the rigid muscles of her shoulders.

For a while, Helen lay still, tense. Then she slowly relaxed. Dane's hands seemed impersonal. He had a good touch, with a strong sense of the body's interconnections.

"Practice what you preach," he ordered gently. "Breathe. Concentrate on the trigger points. That's what you call them, isn't it? Trigger points?"

Helen tried to reply. It was too much work. She murmured something.

"I'll take that as a yes," Dane said. "So concentrate on relaxing. Don't think about anything else."

Instinctively Helen knew that would be a dangerous thing to

do. She tried to hold Josh in her mind, but discovered that was also dangerous. Josh's secret father was here in the room, so close, so strong, so gentle. She dared not think of the child they had made the last time they loved. That prospect had too much allure. Too much danger.

Suddenly the act of making love had a larger meaning than simple pleasure. The pleasure was still there, still overwhelming, but so was that larger meaning.

With a shuddering sigh, Helen pushed Josh out of her mind. But that had its dangers, too. Slowly, she felt her own feelings assert themselves. Slowly she became a woman again, instead of a mother.

And Dane became a man, the magnet for her love.

Beneath his fingers, Dane could feel a subtle change begin in Helen's body. Her bones seemed to soften. There was still tension in her, but it wasn't as harsh. Inevitably he began to think about replacing the tension of wariness with another tension altogether.

Dane tried to concentrate on individual strands of muscle and tried not to think of Helen as a woman. But slowly his stranglehold on his own desire began to weaken. Gradually he felt his body drawn to hers.

The attraction was as powerful as the turning of the seasons. Dane had not consciously set out to seduce Helen; he hadn't needed to be conscious of that. It was as inevitable as breathing.

Helen drew another deep, shuddering breath and let it out slowly.

Dane felt her chest rise as her lungs filled. He let the tips of his fingers stray toward the crease between her arms and the sides of her rib cage. The flesh softened deliciously there. Her arms seemed to move of their own accord, granting him freedom to touch her where he wished. He continued to stroke the muscles, but with each moment, he passed more deeply into her body and her being.

Dane became aware of an annoying roughness beneath his fingers. The sweater. It inhibited him, robbed him of the sensitivity he needed to trace every line of Helen's tension.

"Wait a minute," he whispered softly. "Something keeps getting in the way."

Dane had tugged the hem of the sweater halfway up Helen's body before she realized what he was doing. She stiffened instantly.

"You are wearing something else underneath," he said, laughing softly. "I can feel it. Your modesty is as safe as you want it to be."

Helen tried to lock her arms against her sides, but they seemed weak and useless. Slowly, Dane straightened them out and stretched them above her head so he could remove the sweater.

Soon Helen was wearing only her camisole. She could feel the softness of the fleece above the lacy neckline of her underwear. Warmth radiated from the fire a few feet away. Warmth radiated from Dane.

The sensations were irresistible. Helen surrendered to them, feeling alive again after twenty years, cherished in a way that she never thought she would be again.

Dane's gentleness had pried a small crack in the dam that contained her emotions. Now they began to spill out, powerful and irresistible.

Shivering, Helen savored the touch of Dane's fingers on her bare skin, gently tugging the straps of her camisole aside. But instead of removing it, he left the straps lying loose on her upper arms and went back to work on her shoulders.

Dane's patience seemed inexhaustible. He had begun to understand the nuances of her frame. He bore down with more force and, oddly, more gentleness, smoothing the muscle fibers as though he were molding warm clay. Slowly, muscles softened beneath his fingers.

Just as slowly, one tension was replaced by another kind, as though she was waiting.

Helen drew a deep, ragged breath.

"You learn quickly," she whispered. "Too quickly."

Dane made a noise. His voice was raw. He could not speak. Her waiting was his own. Twenty years of waiting.

Helen sensed the change in Dane's touch. It should have worried her, but it did not. She was vulnerable, immensely vulnerable, but at the moment, nothing in her world could cause her harm.

Dane bore down with his fingers on a long muscle that seemed unusually tight. He felt the muscle tremble for an instant, then release and regain its natural suppleness. One of his hands traced the newly freed band of muscle that radiated out from her spine toward her ribs. Her arms were relaxed now. His fingers traveled down the side of her rib cage and brushed the soft resilience where her breast began.

Helen heard a faint noise far away, quiet and contented, like the sound of a cat in front of a fire. She realized that she had made the noise. She rolled slightly to one side, giving Dane's hand the freedom of her breast.

The soft cry of pleasure came again as Dane's palm slid over Helen's nipple. Slowly he rolled her over on her back and lay down beside her.

For a long time he wouldn't kiss her. He supported himself on one elbow, staring into her eyes and tenderly caressing her breast through the soft cotton of her camisole.

Helen stared back, her dark eyes like bottomless pools gradually refilling with his love. With one hand, she reached across her body and slid the strap of her camisole down. Dane lifted his hand to let the thin fabric fall away. He cupped her bare breast for a moment, then leaned down to brush his lips across her nipple.

Helen lifted herself to him. He caught the rigid point of flesh with his teeth and nipped gently. She moaned and let her head roll to one side. She bit down on her own lower lip, savoring the sensations of being alive again as she had not been alive for twenty years.

The gates of the dam swung open a little more, and emotion spilled out. She felt it run across her lower body. She shivered at its warmth and depth. It reminded her of what she had once been, a raven discovering her wolf, full of certainty, fully wild.

It was a great and inconceivable freedom to be animal again, to be without care, without knowledge of life and death, with only the concentrated awareness of the moment when he would enter her, when they would spin away in the dance that was both death and life.

Finally Dane kissed her lips. Helen reached up to him, drew him down to her. She felt his hands caress her breasts, then slide down her belly and seek the button at the waistband of her skirt. The button slipped through its hole easily. Helen felt the fabric part and glide down over her hips. She lifted herself to help Dane. His palm slid beneath the loosened fabric and covered her wetness.

And then, in a heartbeat, the truth came back to her.

ELEVEN

Helen sat on the rim of the bathtub for a long time, shivering and anguished and struggling desperately to control herself. Finally she straightened her skirt, slipped her sweater back on, and stared at herself in the mirror.

A dark-eyed, tear-streaked, and frightened woman stared back. They regarded each other for a long time. Then Helen turned away, shaking her head in disgust.

She was no coy virgin. She knew all about the power of physical attraction with this one man. She had come home with Dane. She had drunk his wine and eaten his food. She had let him care for her in a way that no man had cared for her, ever. She had let him build a fire from the friction of his hands on her bare skin, on the point of her breast, on the soft flesh of her belly.

Then she had jumped back as though surprised and terrified by the flames.

Helen knew she should not have been surprised to find herself on her back, struggling with her own passion and his, half-drunk on wine and absolutely intoxicated by the man who wanted her so badly his hands shook when he touched her.

Any fool would have expected it to happen, Helen told herself scornfully. Any fool would have stopped the game long before I did. But I let it go on, and it led straight to the brink of disaster.

I can't afford to have Dane in my life. I can't sacrifice Josh's peace of mind for another passionate fling with my wolf.

Helen told herself she had only done what she had to do, but when she looked at her hands again, they still trembled. She had never lain with a man whose physical being so overwhelmed her; she had never wanted a man more than she wanted Dane.

Oh, God, she thought, and what about Dane?

For a second when she had frozen, she thought he might force himself on her. Not that she would have blamed him. She had no right to give him the freedom of her body and then to wrench it away at the last moment. No grown woman would do that to a man and expect him to stop.

She swallowed hard, trying to rid her mouth of the sweetness of his kiss and the bitterness of her ultimate response.

Preferring the mirror to her thoughts, Helen turned back to the unflinching glass. Her hair was tousled from Dane's hands. She tried to push it into place with her fingers. It just got worse.

Finally, she found a brush in a drawer. She lifted it, caught the scent of Dane's shampoo, of Dane. She almost threw the brush at the mirror in frustration. Then she brushed her hair fiercely, until the tears flowed. She gathered her hair at the back of her head and imprisoned it there with a pair of combs from her purse. When she was done, she opened the door again, in control, ready to face Dane's rightful anger.

To Helen's astonishment, Dane was calm. He met her with coffee. There was a dangerous gleam in his eye, a hard male radiance that came of frustration, but he handed the cup to her with a steady hand.

"Drink this," he said. "Then I'll take you back, if you really want that."

Helen accepted the cup carefully, making sure their fingers didn't brush together in the exchange.

"Dane," she said, trying to be precise and controlled.

Her voice broke. She cleared her throat.

"I'm sorry," she said. "I shouldn't have let that happen. It isn't what I want."

Dane's eyes met hers for a moment. She could see that he didn't believe her. His wolf's eyes gleamed with anger, but it was over-whelmed by his gentle, maddening, predatory patience.

"I pushed things too quickly," Dane said. Then he laughed once, sharply. "I wanted you, Helen, just like the first time when I saw you in that pool. I wanted you the same way when I saw you at the woodpile. I won't apologize. I set out to seduce you. Damned near did, too."

He smiled in a blunt, male way.

Helen looked away and struggled with the wild raven who lived in her soul.

Dane took his coffee to the rocking chairs in front of the window, flopped down, and stared out into the dark night.

Without meaning to, Helen padded after him, her bare feet making less noise than the shadow of a raven. She settled in the other chair without looking at him.

The wind had come up. In the light of the setting half-moon, stately old firs tossed like willows, and the surface of the water was like the shattered glass of a quicksilver mirror.

After a moment, Dane shot Helen a sideways look of defiance.

"You wanted me," he said bluntly, angrily. "What happened? Are you punishing me now for twenty years ago?"

Helen closed her eyes. "No. I didn't do this to hurt you. My God, I'm hurting too!"

"Then why did you run away?"

She tried to answer but couldn't find a polite, plausible lie that would draw Dane away from the truth: She couldn't hurt her son to appease her own passions.

"Well?" Dane demanded softly. "Talk to me. I deserve that much, don't you think?"

Helen nodded unhappily.

"Christ, Helen, we're both adults. We both know what this

thing between man and woman is about. We're both free. We're both willing. So what happened?"

There was an odd note in Dane's voice, the beginnings of thought taking root in the turmoil that frustration had made of his mind.

Helen sensed what was happening and froze, like a bird on a nest when a predator is prowling nearby.

"There's more to it than cold feet," Dane said flatly. "What's wrong, Helen? Why won't you give us what we both want until our hands shake?"

"You overwhelmed me," Helen said.

"Bullshit. You were with me every bit of the way until you bolted."

Helen turned and stared out the window again, unable to look at Dane while she told half-truths.

"I'm not used to that kind of passion," she said. "I panicked, that's all. Just panic. Sorry. I feel silly about it."

Dane looked through her with his wolflike eyes. He was not fooled by her words.

Unable to help herself, Helen watched Dane's reflection in the glass of the window. She was both fascinated and horrified by what she saw. He was so controlled, so focused. He still wanted her with an intensity that made her shiver.

His anger would have been so much easier to defeat. She could have been angry in response or she simply could have fled and he wouldn't have had to ask why.

But here they were, bound by a tie neither wanted to break. He was patient and focused, a stalking wolf, and she was drawn to that intensity like a raven on the wing.

She looked away from his reflection in the window.

"Don't," Helen said.

"Don't what?" he asked.

Something snapped inside her.

"Don't look at me like that, you cunning son of a bitch," she snarled.

Dane's eyebrows rose. Then he grinned a little, as though glad to know he wasn't the only one on edge. Leaning forward, he picked up his coffee cup.

And went back to watching Helen.

"What I was trying to say is that I'm the one at fault," she said through her teeth. "I find you attractive as hell. I always have. But I'm thirty-nine years old, I just shipped a son off to school, and I'm in the middle of a very demanding career. I can't handle a serious love affair—and with us, there would be no other kind."

Dane shot Helen a quick, skeptical look. The look told her that he sensed her vulnerability, the young bird in her nest, the secret she must keep at all costs. That rattled her even more.

"Look, let me try and explain it this way," she said, glancing away. "Did you see that brooch I was working on last week, the wax form on my worktable?"

Dane nodded fractionally. "It reminded me of you."

"Yes," Helen said. "It was me, at least partly. I call it *Journey Woman* because that's what I am right now. I'm traveling, moving, changing, free for the first time in my adult life."

She turned and looked squarely at Dane.

"I value my freedom," Helen said distinctly, "just as you once valued yours. You went your own way. I will go mine."

Dane flinched and looked away. "Poetic justice, is that it?"

"I don't know. I do know that we aren't what we were twenty years ago. Our bodies still remember, and with good reason. What we had was incredible. But now we're different."

"It didn't feel different a few minutes ago, when I rolled you over and felt how ready you were to—"

"No!" Helen said, cutting across his words. "That was a mistake. I shouldn't have let it happen. I can't take it back, but I won't let it go on."

"I don't believe you," Dane said. His voice was cool. "I think you want me. Hell, I *know* you want me. And all this crap about being free is just that—crap. We're adults. You can juggle a career and a lover. Or a husband, if that's what you want."

"No," Helen whispered. "Don't, Dane. Please. Don't."

The wind was rising. Helen could hear it now. The branches of a fir tapped eerily on the window, skeleton of a past that refused to be buried.

And everything she did to bury the past deeper only gave it more life.

Dane picked up his cup and drank. Then he stared into the bottom of it, trying to conjure meaning from the dark residue. After a moment, he set the cup aside and walked over to the woman who was watching the night with a raven's clear, unreadable eyes.

"Helen, look at me."

Helen dropped her eyes, studying her hands in her lap.

Finally, Dane crouched in front of her. He put both hands on the arm of her chair, penning her in. He lowered his head until she was forced to look at him.

He nodded slowly.

"Cops see a lot of that look," Dane said. "Secrets hidden behind defiance."

Helen closed her eyes and tried to breathe. She couldn't. Paralyzed, trapped, she waited for the next blow.

"Is that it?" Dane asked gently. "Is there somebody else you don't want to tell me—"

She shook her head violently.

"—about?" Dane continued. "A lover?"

"No."

"Prove it. Touch me and tell me that."

Helen's eyes opened. They were wide, startled.

"I've discovered," Dane said, "that it's damned hard for either of us to lie if we are touching each other."

For a second, Helen sat numbly. Dane was so close to the truth that she couldn't believe he had missed it.

Then she saw a small opening, if only she had enough nerve to take it.

Slowly, Helen reached out with both hands and touched her

palms to Dane's bearded cheeks. Only when she had made that contact did she dare to look directly into his green wolf's eyes.

"I'm not seeing anyone else," she said. "I don't have any secret lovers."

"No. That's too easy."

Dane lifted his hands from the arms of the chair and captured Helen's. He stood up slowly, pulling her up with him. Their bodies touched, melted together. She felt his heartbeat against her breasts and her belly and suddenly realized that Dane was completely aroused.

And completely in control.

Dane draped Helen's hands around his neck and caught her up against him, holding her in the embrace of truth.

By now Helen was so desperate that she was calm. She knew what she must do. She could not lie to Dane, not this way.

"Do you remember that day in the courthouse twenty years ago?" Helen asked.

Dane held her against him. She could feel the rise and fall of his breathing against her breasts. She laid her hands against his chest. She let herself savor the beat of his heart in the flesh that was against her belly.

Dane nodded. "I remember. You said you thought I was wolf to your raven."

"That's an idea from the old stories my mother used to tell, about the wolves and the ravens hunting together. The raven was the scout, leading the wolf to prey. The wolf was the hunter, leaving enough to feed the raven when he was done."

Dane nodded, watching Helen with eyes that saw too much.

"What I was trying to say twenty years ago when I told you to leave," Helen said, "was that I thought we were paired together for all our lives, that we would always hunt like the wolf and the raven of the myths. But I was wrong."

"No. I was the one who was wrong."

Helen stood on tiptoe and brushed her lips over Dane's, silencing him.

"That was a naive young girl talking," Helen said. "Those were a naive young girl's dreams. I'm not that young girl anymore. I have a son, I have a career, I have a world. I could love you again, but it would be like the last time. One night, Dane. Just one."

Dane studied Helen's face, looking for the signs of a lie. He found none, yet he still felt she was concealing a truth that was more important than the one she revealed.

Then Helen's body moved against Dane's, and all that mattered at the moment was that he feel it again. Soon.

"One night?" Dane asked. "You really think you would walk away after one night?"

Helen lifted herself to him again and kissed his lips gently.

"I would have to," she said simply. "It's more than I wanted, probably more than I can handle. . . ."

"Helen," Dane said.

"No, don't say anything. If I don't talk now, I never will."

She put her fingers over Dane's lips. Her eyes shimmered with emotion.

"I wasn't going to go into all this," Helen said. "I was going to see you after I visited Dewey today, and I was going to tell you good-bye. Then you kind of ambushed me back there."

For the first time, Helen smiled. "Actually, you don't deserve all the blame."

She let her hands slide down Dane's chest. Still in the circle of his arms, she put her hands behind her and brushed the tops of his knuckles with her fingers.

"You can't be blamed for having such wonderful hands," Helen said, and her smile became almost shy. "You made a shambles of my good intentions."

Dane caught Helen's hands in his own and held them lightly. Her gesture had heightened the pressure of her body against his own. He drew her into a maddeningly intimate embrace, his decision made.

"I've never felt like much of a lover with anybody but you," Dane said.

He kissed her.

Pinned against him, her hands captured and helpless behind her own body, Helen did not resist. She simply let herself go. This was the dangerous choice she had made. She would distract Dane with the only bait at hand. Herself.

Dane's kiss changed, no longer gentle. He arched her against his body, blind with hunger and overflowing with desire. Helen strained against him, shivering violently with a passion that had waited twenty years to be freed.

"What I love is your wildness," Dane said. "I won't take that from you. But I can't let you go tonight."

"Tonight. Just tonight."

Instead of answering, Dane kissed Helen on the lips and then on eyes that were bright with passion or sorrow or both. He opened the circle of his arms and offered her his hand. When she took it, he led her toward the stairs.

As Helen let Dane guide her up the stairs, she sealed her son away in the far part of her mind.

Dane undressed her with infinite care, as though he were uncovering a masterpiece that had been heavily wrapped and laid away for twenty years. Then she undid his clothing, savoring the dark hair of his chest and the blunt, potent flesh she had not allowed herself to think about for twenty years.

They lay down on the bed together, drawing around themselves the silver blackness of the raven's mystery and the elemental reality of the wolf.

They loved until they were exhausted, then they slept together beneath a down comforter, holding to each other as though each was counting off the seconds of the night as it slid toward dawn.

Just before five A.M., the phone downstairs rang.

Dewey was dying.

TWELVE

The first faint light of day outlined the peaks of the North Cascades as Dane pulled onto the lonely highway, headed for town. Helen stared out the side window at the remnants of the night. She had slept little. Her dark eyes were hollow with exhaustion.

Dane fiddled with the heater, trying to milk some warmth from it. The air was cold, and Helen was still dressed for a fall afternoon, but she had refused his offer of a coat.

Dane watched the eastern skyline take shape. "It will be a good day," he said, "not the kind of day Dewey would choose to die. Maybe the nurse was wrong."

Helen shook her head without looking at Dane. "Dawn is a good time to die. I think Dewey is ready."

"Did he tell you that?" Dane asked.

She nodded. "I could feel it in his body. I think the pain is over but he's very tired. He's ready to be free."

Dane listened to Helen's words and knew she was right, although a part of him still rejected the idea.

"I guess so," Dane said, "but . . . "

He stopped, grappling with a thought that had not crystallized.

Helen waited and watched him with a raven's dark eyes.

"Dewey is the only person alive who knew me as a child," Dane said softly, surprised that he had just found words to describe his feeling.

For a second, he felt the tears well up again, as they had in the hallway of the nursing home. He swallowed hard and tried to quell them.

Helen touch Dane's arm with her hand. "It's okay to cry."

Dane didn't reply, stubbornly hanging on to his feelings.

Helen broke the physical contact between them and shifted on the seat, as though she were bracing herself and ordering her emotions. She was more experienced at this sort of thing than he was.

"You would do better to cry now rather than when you see Dewey," she said.

Dane stared at the roadway ahead, still fighting for self-control. "Why?"

"Dewey is ready to die. The kindest thing we can do for him is to let go of him. Your tears will make him fight to hang on to life. He loves you. He wants to make things as easy as he can on you. Yet he is dying, and he knows it. Let him go, Dane. He is very tired."

Dane drove on silently for a time, caught in his own emotions. Suddenly he found himself staring into the headlights of an oncoming car. He swerved back into his own lane reflexively and pulled to the side of the road.

Once he stopped, Dane realized that his hands ached. He had been gripping the wheel as though it were the last scrap of his childhood. He swallowed hard and felt a shuddering sigh pass through him, as though he were finally able to let go, now that he understood the cost of hanging on. He rested his arms on the steering wheel and put his head down on them. The tears he had fought so hard finally flowed freely and without shame.

Helen felt the urge to touch him again, to stroke the back of his strong hand, to test the resilience of the muscles in his forearm with her fingers, to reassure him that they were both still alive. But she fought the urge. It would only bring her closer to the brink of disaster. It was less binding to share sex with Dane than it would be to share grief.

Dane straightened up slowly and stared out into the dark woods that had begun to take shape beside the road. He brushed his index finger past both of his eyes, wiping away the last of his tears.

Then he gazed out through the windshield at the false dawn and laid his hand, palm up, on the bench seat between them.

Helen tried to ignore the offer of his hand but found she could not. She put her hand inside Dane's. He wrapped his fingers firmly around hers and held on.

"I'm not used to this," he said huskily. "It's new to me, all of it. I have no right to ask, but will you . . . will you help me with this?"

He felt her hand turn cold and sensed that she wanted to withdraw.

"Not just for me," he added. "For Dewey, too."

Helen saw the moment more clearly than he did. Dane's request was somehow more vital, more binding, than a marriage proposal. He was asking her to share his pain, the meat and blood of his life.

Helen was no stranger to deathbeds. She had sat at more of them than she wanted to remember. Dying was a process she understood at some elemental level, and she had shared that understanding with others many times.

But Dane and Dewey were not merely two men facing a critical moment in both of their lives. They were too close to her.

They both had Josh's green, watchful wolf's eyes.

"Dane," Helen said helplessly, "I don't . . . I don't think it's my place."

"I need you," Dane said.

He stopped, suddenly surprised at the intensity and truth of his own words.

"I don't want to put too much pressure on you," he said. "I don't have that right. But I do need you. I'm just beginning to realize how much."

Helen pulled her hand from Dane's grip and sat staring out through the windshield.

"I thought we had an agreement," she said, grappling with the dread that had lain just beneath her consciousness all night long, even as she let him hold her both safe and threatened in his arms.

Dane started to say something, then caught himself. "I guess we did. But I thought somehow last night would change how you felt. I know it changed me. This is the wrong time and the wrong place, Helen, but I—"

"No!" Helen interrupted swiftly. "Don't say it or I swear I'll get out of this truck right now."

She wrapped her arms around herself and shivered, as though the cold had suddenly penetrated her flesh and settled in her bones.

"Oh, God, this is such a mess," she said. "I never should have let you touch me. I never should have let it happen, not twenty years ago and not last night."

Dane felt a rising sense of fear. "I've played all my cards faceup. Twenty years ago, I would have done anything to have you for a night. Now, I'm not interested in one night. I'm—"

"No!"

Helen's vehemence was shocking. It stunned both of them. Dane stared at her, trying to understand.

"I'm sorry, Dane," she said, her voice softer. "I know you're being honest, and I want to be as honest with you as I can be."

She groped for convincing words. She could not lie to him, but the game of half-truth and misdirection became more difficult and more dangerous with each moment she was close to her wolf.

"Dane, this is the truth. Last night was something that shouldn't have happened but I will thank God until my dying day that it did.

"You are the most extraordinary man I've ever known, the most extraordinary man I will ever know. *But I won't love you.* I won't let myself, and I'm not even going to try to explain why.

You'll never understand, not really. There is simply too much between us . . . and not enough. It was always that way."

Helen drew a deep, ragged breath and spoke again, calmer now.

"It ends here, Dane. I won't come into the hospital with you."

There was a tense silence, then Dane looked away.

"You still hate me," he said. "I shouldn't be surprised, I guess. But I am. There's so much generosity in you . . . for other people."

Helen knew she should say nothing and let Dane believe the lie he had spoken. Yet she couldn't. The pain in his voice and in his empty hand clenched on the seat between them was too great.

"I don't hate you," Helen said shakily. "Every time we are together, every time we eat or watch a sunset or make love, something extraordinary happens. We are dragged deeper and deeper into a place where neither one of us can stay.

"You know that and I know it, but the same damned thing just keeps happening, over and over. Somehow it's got to stop, so I'll stop it because I'm the one who started it a long, long time ago."

Helen turned toward Dane and saw her wolf watching her with hope and wariness and pain in his eyes.

"It's over, Dane," she said harshly. "Our love never should have been and never will be. Accept that, or we'll both regret what follows until we die."

Dane gripped the wheel with both hands again, stunned by Helen's vehemence and the naked pain in her voice. Part of him felt a crushing anguish, part a numb confusion. He had never cared for another human being the way he did for Helen. That made her obvious pain all the more difficult for him to bear.

Finally, Dane drew a deep breath and blew it out slowly, trying to dispel his confusion with the air he breathed. He looked at Helen. She sat with her eyes closed and her head lowered, almost as though she were waiting for a blow.

"All right," he said softly. "I hear you. I don't understand but I do hear you. I've given you and yours all the pain either of us can handle, so I'll stop. If it helps, I'm sorry as hell about it, and I'll be sorry until the day I die. Longer, likely. That's what hell is all about, isn't it?"

Dane's soft, gentle voice was not what Helen expected. It almost undid her. She began crying. Her shoulders shook with silent sobs. For a long time, she couldn't speak.

Finally, she did. "Thank you."

"And good-bye?"

"Yes," Helen whispered.

Without a word Dane turned the truck out onto the road again. They rode silently the rest of the way to the hospital. Helen pointed to her car sitting alone in what had been a crowded parking lot, and Dane pulled up beside it. She fumbled blindly for the door handle on the truck and opened it.

She was already halfway out, ready to flee, when Dane's hand shot out and his fingers wrapped around her arm. She was stiff and inflexible. She refused to look back at him.

"This isn't the time for the living to say good-bye to each other. I'll come see you after Dewey dies."

Helen shook her head. She would have ordered him to stay away, but she didn't trust her own voice.

"I won't give you any more pain," Dane said, "that much I promise. I love you, raven."

Helen made a broken sound and wrenched free. Dane watched her get in the car and drive away without looking back.

Suddenly he was as spent as if he had run a marathon. He released the brake and coasted across the empty lot to a spot near the front door of the hospital.

The nurse at the aid station outside Dewey's room looked relieved when Dane walked down the hall.

"They brought him over from the nursing home about three, but he's slipping fast," she said. "They're just getting ready to move him to the intensive care ward."

"No!"

Dane's response was so sharp that the nurse flinched as though she had been slapped.

"No intensive care," Dane said evenly, "no heroic measures. Let him die in peace."

THIRTEEN

Dewey lay on his right side, his legs drawn up like a child's. His eyes were open and there was a fixed expression on his face. He was concentrating on something only he could see. He drew quick, shallow breaths, as though his lungs had turned to cardboard.

Quietly, Dane closed the door of the room behind him and went to the side of the bed.

"Hi, Dewey," he said softly. "Feel like a visitor?"

The glazed expression slowly faded from Dewey's eyes. What could have been a smile passed over his gaunt features, but he said nothing.

Dane put his hand on Dewey's bony shoulder and squeezed gently. The old man's body was cool beneath the thin cotton hospital gown. Dane pulled the blanket up and tucked it around Dewey's shoulders.

"How's that?" Dane asked. "Can I get you something?"

Dewey's lips moved but little sound came. Dane leaned down and put his ear close to Dewey's mouth.

"Water," was the word Dewey was trying to say.

Dane found a glass of water and straw on the bedside table. He gently lifted the old man's head and slipped the plastic straw between his lips. Dewey drew on the straw, but he was so weak he couldn't pull the water up the straw to his mouth.

"Wait," Dane said.

He set the glass down, laid the straw aside, and gathered Dewey in one arm. He lifted the frail man and brought the water glass to his lips.

Dewey sipped at the water several times like a bird. And like a bird, he tilted his head back, letting gravity do the work of swallowing. After another sip, he made a sound that meant that he had drunk enough.

Dane laid his uncle back on the pillow but stayed close, bent over the bed protectively, holding Dewey's bony hand gently between his own much warmer palms.

The water seemed to clear Dewey's throat. He was able to make words.

"Helen?" he asked.

"She, uh, couldn't come. It's the middle of the night yet, for most people."

Dewey thought awhile about that, then nodded an inch in acknowledgment. His eyes searched the room and finally lit on the heavy vase of dahlias that someone had thought to bring with him from the nursing home.

"Say . . . " he whispered laboriously, ". . . thanks. For flowers. Everything."

Dane nodded. "I'll tell her. She was pleased that you liked them."

Dewey was quiet for a moment, but Dane sensed a tension, as though the old man was gathering his strength.

"She is wise," Dewey finally said, his voice raspy yet clear.

Dane nodded, unable to speak.

"She said we have . . . same eyes," Dewey whispered. "Did she tell you about . . . about eyes?"

"No. I guess she forgot. Now rest a bit."

A chuckle rattled deep in Dewey's throat.

"Why? Why rest? Real rest soon enough."

The ghost child inside the old man flashed a little grin that was heartbreaking in its impish innocence.

Dane grinned back despite the ache in his throat. "I guess you're right. Talk as much as you want."

Dewey nodded a slow inch, but the effort seemed to exhaust him. He lay back on the pillow and stared past Dane toward the opposite wall.

They were silent together for a time. Then Dane sensed that Dewey's eyes had fixed on something. He followed the old man's line of sight and saw the faint orange of dawn outlining the drawn drapes of the hospital room.

"Would you like to see the light?" Dane asked.

Dewey responded with a weak squeeze of his nephew's hand.

Dane was opening the drapes when the nurse stuck her head into the room.

"Those should be left closed," she said. "The light will be right in his eyes."

"That's the whole idea," Dane said curtly.

The nurse looked at Dewey, who was watching the drapes open with the curious intensity of the dying. She withdrew, closing the door behind her.

Dane felt faintly guilty about barking at the poor woman. She was only doing her job. But all of them, the doctors and nurses, looked upon death as a failure. That was not only wrong, it was foolish. Doctors could postpone death, delay it, and stretch out the process of dying. But they could not reverse it.

Dane wished to hell they weren't so eager to try. Helen had been right. Dewey was ready to die. Dane could see it in his uncle's eyes, sense it in the cool frailty of his body.

What better time than now? What better way than into the sunrise?

When the drapes were fully open, Dane went back to the bed and took the old man's hand. Together, they watched the sky brighten behind the jagged ridges of the Cascades.

Slowly, just as the sun appeared behind the craggy black peaks, Dane felt Dewey's hand loosen. The old man began to slide away, his eyes fixed on the clean, yellow light.

Then Dewey seemed to flinch and draw back. His fingers wrapped around Dane's hand, and he held on, struggling to return.

Dane remembered what Helen had said.

"It's okay, Dewey. I'll miss you. But everything is taken care of here."

Dane swallowed hard and drew a deep breath.

"You're free to go," Dane said in a clear, gentle voice. "I love you."

Slowly, gently, the fingers that had built a house and written biology lessons on a blackboard and fished and loved and wiped away Dane's tears . . . slowly the gnarled old fingers went slack.

This time Dewey did not struggle. This time he flew away, away, away, and it was to light he flew, not darkness.

The last breath spilled slowly out of Dewey's tired lungs. Dane saw wrinkled old eyelids slide down over wolf-green eyes for the last time. He started to release his hold on Dewey's hand when he realized the process was not over.

There was still some quiet spirit inside the body. That spirit was at peace, but it needed to linger awhile, like the last ember of a fire burning out in its own way, in its own time.

Dane held on to Dewey's hand, watching, listening with his own inner ear, waiting until he felt himself to be truly alone in the room. He had no idea how long it took. He knew only that the time gave him a profound sense of peace, reminding him of a line he had heard in church a long, long time ago, about a peace that surpassed all understanding.

Gently, Dane folded Dewey's hands across the now still chest. He sat on a chair by the bed, watching the soaring light behind the granite mountains.

The peace of that sunrise taught Dane that some things in life were much worse than death.

FOURTEEN

On a dark, drizzly afternoon a week later, Dane nosed Dewey's cabin cruiser into a dock at the Raven Island Marina. He shut down the little diesel engine, stepped onto the wet dock, and threw a quick loop of the bow line over a cleat.

The tide was slack, allowing the stern of the boat to swing obediently against the dock. Dane tied off the boat against the bumpers with a short line.

There was something melancholy about the clean-lined wooden boat's willingness. Dewey had fished from it every summer for more than thirty years. Now it had just borne his ashes out onto the waters of Langley Channel.

The boat was like a faithful old dog who had outlived its master. Dane had no room for it in his life, and salmon fishermen in the sound now favored fiberglass hulls with inboard gasoline engines. Dane had been reduced to selling Dewey's boat to a marine contractor from Langley who needed something to haul construction material and dredged sand.

Dane knew what that meant. In five years, maybe less, the clean white boat would be a dirty, punched-out hull without salvage value, without history, without sentimental or practical worth.

Unhappily, Dane stared at the green block letters on the white bow. The *Beagle*. The name was a gesture of respect for Charles

Darwin, but it was also a gentle biologist's dig at local fundamentalist Christians. For years, they had tried to force Dewey to teach "creationist science" in his biology classes. For years, Dewey had fought. Now his ongoing act of defiance would be lost in the static of everyday life.

Hell, I'm probably the only one who gets that joke anymore, Dane thought. Not that it matters. It all comes to ashes and dust in the end.

He told himself that the gray day and the scattering of Dewey's ashes were responsible for his grim mood, but that was a lie, and he knew it. He had kept himself busy for a week with his duties as Dewey's executor and sole survivor. He had disposed of the ashes according to the will, and he had sold the boat. Now there was one last bitter duty.

Dane lifted the collar of his coat against the rain and headed down the dock for the paved road that cut across the center of Raven Island.

The windows of the little cabin on the beach were dark, as though no one was there, but as Dane turned into the yard, he smelled wood smoke from the fireplace.

He knocked on the door. When there was no answer, he turned the knob and stuck his head in.

"Helen?"

No reply. He sniffed the air, then checked the stove. A pot of bean soup bubbled slowly on the burner. Helen would not be far away.

Dane went back into the front yard and walked easily up the big boulder at the edge of the sand. From the top of the boulder, Dane could see a woman walking the surf line in a black cape. Two ravens swirled like huge black leaves around her.

As Dane watched, Helen bent over and inspected a scattered fan of rocks at the edge of the growling surf. One of the ravens landed nearby and hopped over, as though to help in a search. Dane wondered whether the bird was Thought or Memory.

He stood in the dripping weather for a while, plotting his

course. He had come, as he promised, to say good-bye. He did not expect to change Helen's mind. She had made it clear that she didn't want him in her life.

Sometimes Dane wasn't sure he blamed her. Sometimes the twin ravens of thought and memory were blessing, and sometimes they were curse.

But Dane wanted the farewell to be more of a healing than another wounding. He wanted to avoid the frustration and anger that had haunted both of them for twenty years.

The rain continued to fall. Dane thought about walking out to meet Helen on the beach but decided against it. He retreated to the house to wait for her.

Once inside, he turned on a few lights as a gentle warning to Helen. He took off his slicker and was shaking it on the hearth in front of the fire when the phone rang.

Dane waited, expecting an answering machine to pick up the call, but nothing happened. At ten, the rings stopped. Then, a few seconds later, they started all over.

That kind of persistence hinted at importance. Dane picked up the black phone on the worktable.

"This is Helen Raven's residence," he said.

There was a hesitation on the line. Dane could hear the faint hum of long distance in the silence, then a young man's voice.

"Uh, hi, this is Josh. Is my mother there?"

Dane suddenly realized that he was still holding his dripping coat. He shifted the receiver to his other ear and tossed the slicker over the back of a chair.

"She's out front, down the beach about a quarter mile. I can get her for you, but it would take a couple of minutes."

"Damn," Josh said.

"Want me to have her call you back?"

"I'm not in the dorm, so she can't call me back easily."

Then, as though it had just occurred to Josh, he asked, "Who is this, anyway?"

There was a faint challenge in his voice, telling Dane that Josh was used to acting as his mother's protector, whether she needed it or not.

No sense in alarming the kid, Dane told himself. Even at eighteen, he probably still had a hard time with his mother's boyfriends or lovers.

"My name is Dane Corvin. I knew your mother a couple of years before you were born."

"Really? Cool. Do you live on Raven Island?"

"No. I just came back to see my uncle."

"Corvin? Oh, yeah, Mom said something about your uncle being sick. He taught as a substitute in my biology class. Say hi to him for me. Maybe he'll remember me. I was the one who taught Thought and Memory to speak."

Dane hesitated, then spoke. "Dewey died four days ago."

The boy's response was quick and genuine.

"I'm sorry. He was a good teacher."

"One of the best," Dane said, "in or out of the classroom."

"He was always after the class, and me in particular. 'Use your eyes, boy,' he said over and over. 'They're unusual eyes. Put them to work.'"

Slowly, Dane breathed through the pain of Dewey's loss.

"I think about him sometimes when I pick up my camera," Josh continued. "Cameras are just another way of looking at things."

"I'm sure Dewey would have enjoyed knowing that."

"Oh, he did," Josh said. "I ran into him last summer, just before I left for the East. I told him exactly what I just told you."

Dane found himself wondering why Dewey had not mentioned that meeting.

"Did your mother know about that?" he asked, trying to sound offhanded.

"She was with me when I saw Mr. Corvin. Didn't she ever tell you?"

"No, no she didn't. But then, I haven't been around her all that long."

"Have you seen Thought and Memory?" Josh asked eagerly.

"They're with her right now on the beach."

"They must be hunting agates," Josh said, sounding a little wistful. "Ravens have great eyes for the shiny stones. Thought likes blue-whites, and Memory is a killer for the champagne browns."

Dane's eye was drawn to the jar of agates on the windowsill in Helen's studio. He had seen them the first time he was here, but hadn't paid much attention.

"Blue-whites? Champagnes?" Dane asked. "Makes them sound like diamonds," he said.

"That comes of being raised by an artist, I guess. Mom's got a name for every color you've ever seen."

The wistful note came again. Dane wondered if Josh was homesick. Harvard was a long, long way from Raven Island.

"Homesick?" Dane asked gently.

"At first I really was. I felt as lost as I did when Dad died. Then I met, uh, some people and . . . "

Dane smiled as Josh's voice faded. He suspected that Josh was still homesick and reluctant to admit it.

"Well, you'll be back home soon for Thanksgiving," Dane said.

"Uh, that's what I was calling about."

Dane made an encouraging sound.

"I decided to save my ticket money for a Christmas surprise," Josh said quickly. "With any luck, I'll be back by December fifteenth. I'd better be. Mom's probably about out of wood."

Dane laughed out loud. Maybe the kid wasn't such a spoiled prince, after all.

"Don't worry," Dane said. "She'll do fine until Christmas."

"Oh, good. I felt bad about that." Josh hesitated, then plunged ahead with the bluntness of youth. "Are you going to be there for Thanksgiving?"

Dane was equally blunt. "No."

"Damn. I hate to think of Mom being alone. If I know her, she'll probably get involved in some project and forget all about eating, much less about cooking a turkey. But if I come home now, it will really louse up my Christmas plans."

Dane heard a voice close by the other end of the line. A girl's voice, but indistinct.

"Listen," Josh said, "someone's waiting. I've got to go. Tell Mom I called, and I'll call her again on Thanksgiving."

"I'll give her the message."

"And I'm sorry about Mr. Corvin. I liked him."

Josh hung up and was gone, leaving Dane with a vague feeling of disappointment. He had enjoyed talking to the boy about Dewey and Thought and Memory.

For a moment longer, Dane stood with the phone in his hand, thinking about his own student days. When he was around Josh's age, he had skipped Thanksgiving at home, too, just to go skiing. A month later, his parents had been killed.

Even after twenty-two years, the pain of that holiday could still sting like a salt-tipped whip, as fresh as Dewey's loss.

Josh is a decent kid, Dane thought. Helen misses him a lot. Neither of them deserves a holiday alone. There will be plenty of those later on.

Dane tapped the phone hook until he got a dial tone. Then he punched in an 800 number he knew by heart. The drill was a familiar one: Dane had reached into his wallet for a credit card even before the airline ticket agent got on the line.

Helen spotted the lights in the house while she was still a hundred yards down the beach. She had been expecting Dane for several days, ever since she had read Dewey's obituary in the town paper.

There had been a memorial service at the local high school, but Helen had stayed away, unable to face Dane and hating herself for it. Now he had come, as he had promised he would.

Helen steeled herself for one last meeting, hoping she would not have to drive him off with anger or hatred. She wasn't sure she could do that again. She was only sure that he must be gone before Josh came home for Thanksgiving.

When Helen entered the house, Dane was standing by the

hearth, his back to the fire. He looked tired and drawn, but he managed a smile.

"I had Dewey's boat out for one last run in the channel and thought I'd stop by," Dane said. "I'll be leaving tomorrow."

Helen bit back her instinctive protest at losing Dane again. She pulled the damp wool hood of her cape off her head and undid the catch at her throat. Her hair was damp on her forehead, and she suddenly felt chilled beyond hope of warming.

"You look as tired as I feel," Dane said.

The dark circles under Helen's eyes gave her skin an ivory cast. Dane felt a twinge of guilt. She looked as if she had suffered more in the last week than he had.

"Did you find any agates?" he asked gently.

Helen looked surprised. "How did you know that's what I was doing?"

"Josh told me. He called while you were out."

Helen's face lost all its color. *"You talked to Josh?"*

Dane nodded.

"Why?" she asked starkly.

Dane watched Helen uneasily, beginning to wish he had not come. Everything he did or said seemed only to deepen her distress. That wasn't what he wanted. He wanted . . . peace. For both of them.

"I wouldn't have answered your phone, but he tried twice in a row," Dane said. "I thought it might be something serious. But it wasn't. I think he was just homesick."

Helen let out a long breath.

"You really ought to get an answering machine," Dane said. "Even hermit artists need to stay in touch."

Helen stared at the phone on her desk as though it had betrayed her.

"Listen," Dane said, "I did something that was probably none of my business. Josh was going to save the cost of his Thanksgiving ticket for some kind of Christmas surprise, and I knew you were missing him, so . . . "

Helen heard Dane's words faintly, as though they were coming across a vast distance. True father and hidden son had met. They had spoken more than casually. Her worst fear had been realized, yet her secret was still intact.

"... I called an airline and arranged for a prepaid ticket in his name. Just think of it as a last bequest from Dewey, and act surprised when Christmas comes and he springs whatever it is on you and you wonder where he got the money. Okay?"

Helen wasn't listening. She felt her skin draw tight, as though it were shrinking on her, squeezing her until she could barely breathe.

Josh talked to a father he doesn't even know exists, Helen thought. Dane talked to a son he can't even imagine.

Dewey died without knowing he had a great-nephew, another Corvin to look out on the world with a wolf's wild and shrewd green eyes.

Dane could die tomorrow. He could die forty years from now. *And he would never know he had a son.*

Helen wrapped her arms around her body and trembled, wondering how she would live with herself. It was one thing to conceal a son from the Dane of twenty years ago, a confident young wolf who had met her truth with deceit, had enjoyed a one-night stand with her, and had gone on to the rest of his life with few regrets, if any.

But it was another thing to hide a son from the Dane she knew now, a man who kept nothing of the truth from her, a man who knew his own mortality, a man whose eyes darkened with pain whenever he talked about the future; the end of the Corvin line. Of himself.

Yet it wouldn't be the end. Not while Josh lived, and Josh's children, and his children's children.

Dane wouldn't know that unless she told him.

"Oh, God," Helen whispered in agony, not even knowing she spoke aloud.

Unhappily, Dane watched her. She was as still and pale as

death. He sensed her turmoil, scented her fear, and thought it was for her son.

"Josh just needed to talk to you," Dane said. "He's only, what, barely eighteen? It's his first time away from home. Don't worry about him. He's much stronger than you think. After all, he's your son."

Helen stared across the room at the desk, listening to her own words rather than Dane's.

Is Josh old enough now to know? she asked herself. Can he accept the truth and not hate me for lying to him even after Ted died?

Will there be no end to the pain of a mistake I made twenty years ago?

What am I to do?

"Helen?"

Finally, slowly, Helen focused on Dane. She stared into his pale green eyes, seeing compassion and grief, pain and loneliness . . . and a love for her that cut her heart out.

In that moment, Helen knew she might still drive Dane away. With the right words, she could make sure that he would never return. Ever. The agonizing secret would remain intact. In her mind, she even heard the words she needed to say: Good-bye, Dane.

Those few words would protect her from Josh's anger and scorn and even, possibly, hatred. Those words would protect Josh's sense of his childhood, of himself.

Those words would protect everyone, but at the cost of the man who loved her.

She opened her mouth but could not bring herself to say the magic words. They were too painful, too final, too much like the sound of graveside dirt flung onto a coffin.

I can't speak, she realized. I can't remain silent. I can't continue to torment the fully grown wolf whose only mistake is to love a raven far more foolish than she is wise.

"Helen?" Dane reached toward her, then dropped his hand when she flinched. "Are you all right?"

Without answering, Helen slowly walked across the room to her desk.

Dane watched her uneasily. She moved as though wading against invisible currents. She reached into a glass bowl and pulled out a heavy antique key. The key fit into the lock of the middle desk drawer. There was a subdued click. The drawer slid open.

Helen stared for a long moment at the picture that lay face-down in its metal frame, hidden since the day Dane had walked back into her life. With a bittersweet smile, she picked up the picture, held it to her breasts for a moment, then stepped away from the desk and walked back across the room toward Dane.

She looked at him and remembered what he had told her about nearly striking the woman who had aborted his seed. What would he do to the woman who had given birth to his son—*and hidden that son from him?*

Grief deepened in Helen. For a few more moments, she savored the love and concern in Dane's eyes, fearing she was seeing them for the last time. Then she spoke.

"Nearly twenty," Helen said softly.

Dane shook his head slowly, confused.

"What?"

"You said you thought Josh was eighteen, but he'll be twenty in April. He was so upset when Ted died that he missed a year of school."

Then Helen handed Dane the framed self-portrait of Josh with Thought and Memory.

Dane stared at a handsome young man with dark hair like Helen's. A young man with the striking, slightly Asian features that were often a product of the mixing of European and Indian blood.

And then Dane saw something else—cool, amused green eyes that were like Dewey's, eyes that were like his father's, eyes that were like Dane's.

His head snapped up.

"Yes," Helen said. "Josh is your son. Those damned, beautiful wolf's eyes."

FIFTEEN

Dane felt as though he had grabbed a live wire in his hand. Recognition raced through the center of his body. He was paralyzed, caught in the grip of a force that was too powerful to fight. He braced himself against the pain that he knew would come when the shock passed.

Josh's smile was off-center and lively. Dane thought he saw a bit of his own mother in it. He hadn't seen her face clearly in his mind for years, but now she was there in her grandson, as clear as if he had seen her yesterday.

His father was there, too, in those green eyes and that level gaze.

Dane wondered at genetic power. He also wondered what his parents would have made of this handsome young man who tamed ravens and went to Harvard.

Then the rest of the emotions flooded through Dane's mind— rage, humiliation, fear, joy, confusion. But strongest was the rage at all he had lost of his own son's life.

Dane looked at Helen. She was motionless, watching him with dark, frightened eyes.

"Well, I guess we're even now, once and for all," Dane said.

His voice was soft, nearly a whisper, but Helen flinched at the fury it contained. Then anger came to her, freeing her from fear.

"Do you really think that's what this is about?" she demanded.

Dane shrugged, indifferent to other possibilities.

"Well, then, why don't you just hit me and get it over with?" Helen asked mockingly.

"Hit you?" Dane sounded as though the idea hadn't occurred to him.

"That's right, that's what you nearly did to the woman who had an abortion," Helen said. "Which is worth more, an aborted child or a son whose childhood you've missed, a son who doesn't even know you exist?"

Dane simply watched Helen through narrowed green eyes.

"Who betrayed you more deeply?" Helen demanded. "Which one of us deprived you of a bigger portion of your manhood? I need to know. Obviously, I *still* don't understand the male psyche."

Dane didn't trust himself to speak, to move, to do anything more than stare at the woman who had betrayed him with a cruelty he was still learning.

Helen spun away and stared out the window at the falling rain. Her shoulders shook with anger or sobs. Finally, slowly, she began to regain her composure. She looked back at Dane, her eyes filled with bitter tears.

"If you think I did this to get even with you," she said savagely, "you know even less about motherhood than about fatherhood!"

"What am I supposed to do? Tell me, Helen, I'm not used to this new role. Most guys get at least nine months."

"You had twenty years," she shot back, her voice an indictment of all men.

"But no way of knowing!"

"Didn't the possibility ever occur to you? Not even once?"

Dane shook his head emphatically. "Not once. Your charade was damned good. You must have gotten quite a thrill, staring me right in the face, there in the courthouse, and lying to me like a lawyer."

"I didn't know I was pregnant," Helen said bitterly. "Not then, not until later. You still aren't very good at math, are you?"

"Not nearly as good as you are at lying."

"Listen to you, the wolf who lied his way into my brother's heart and my soul."

Wounded and proud, so caught up in themselves they could not see the other's pain, Helen and Dane stared furiously at each other.

"Tell me the truth about something," Dane finally said. "How much did Dewey know about this?"

He watched Helen narrowly, as though afraid of what she might say. Or not say.

"Dewey knew whatever he guessed the first time he saw Josh," Helen said.

"You didn't put him up to it?"

The implications of the question dawned slowly. Helen shook her head.

"Don't worry," she said coolly. "Dewey didn't betray you, because I didn't tell him a damned thing. He saw Josh in class that first day and recognized him. Those damned wolf's eyes."

Dane nodded slowly.

"So Dewey checked the school records," Helen said, "did a little detective work, and came up with a great-nephew he never knew he had. He decided to call you. He decided to bring you back. He wanted you to know you had a son. He hoped you and I . . . " Helen closed her eyes. "Anyway, he ran out of strength before he could pull it off."

"If you weren't in on it with Dewey, how do you know so much?"

"Oh, come on, Dane. I can add three and two and get five. Dewey knew Josh. Dewey knew he was dying. Dewey knew you had never married. He knew I had never remarried. He wanted us to be a family."

"And you didn't." Dane's voice was a lot calmer than his eyes.

"I wanted Josh to have a less savage transition from childhood to adulthood than I did," Helen said flatly. "I didn't want his sense of who he was to be destroyed between one breath and the next, the way mine was. I nearly went under, Dane. It was close, so damned close."

Dane's eyes widened in shock. He had always thought of Helen as strong, almost invulnerable, a raven soaring on the wind.

"Anyway," Helen said, "I didn't bring you back to sleep with you and then make your life living hell because you had done the same to me twenty years ago. Until this afternoon, until a moment ago, I was going to say good-bye without telling you."

"Why didn't you do that?" Dane asked. "Christ, woman, another ten minutes and I'd have been gone!"

"And you would have died not knowing you had a son," Helen said. "You would have died believing you were the last of your kind. No matter what you had done to me as a girl, I couldn't do that to you as a woman."

The bitter truth in Helen's voice shocked Dane from his rage. He tried to speak but couldn't find anything to say now that anger was no longer driving him.

"Poor Josh," Helen said finally. "What a mess we both made of his childhood."

Dane glanced at the picture that was still in his hands. The boy's crooked smile was innocent, without guile.

"Yeah, I guess he's got a lot of growing up to do real quick," Dane said.

Helen closed her eyes against the pain. "You're going to tell him."

"Of course," Dane said. No other possibility had occurred to him.

"When? How? On the phone?"

Dane stared at the picture for a long time. Then he handed it back to Helen.

"Thanksgiving," Dane said. "I want to be with him when he learns who his father really was."

"His father *really* was Ted Hartel in all but one way! Have you thought about that? Have you thought about what telling Josh will do to him?"

EVAN MAXWELL

"Everybody grows up sometime."

Helen held the picture to herself as though it were an infant while she watched Dane pull on his coat.

"It's not just his childhood you'll be destroying," she said. Then Helen handed Dane the picture of Josh. "We both know you could destroy me in his eyes. It would be a suitable revenge, wouldn't it?"

Dane accepted the photo without a word.

"Then remember," Helen whispered, "that you may well destroy yourself at the same time."

Helen turned away and went to the hearth. She stood staring at the fire until she heard Dane close the door behind him as he left.

SIXTEEN

Dane pulled his truck into Dewey's garage as the cold gray rain turned to a stinging mixture of snow and hail the size of frozen white rice.

Dane got out of the truck, put the picture beneath his jacket, and stood in the weather for a long time, letting the hard white pellets strike his face. The wind sighed through the last flat green leaves of the madrone beside the garage. The rustling of the leaves was a sound made by a thousand unhappy memories.

He had a son, an heir, an extension of himself and his ancestors. Until that moment, he had not admitted to himself how much that meant.

Christ, he thought, a week ago I was even wondering if Helen was still fertile, whether we might even start our own belated family.

That question had now become moot in the most remarkable way, yet Dane was as lonely as he had ever been in his life. He stood in the growing storm until he began to shiver from the cold. Only then did he go inside and build a fire.

The bright flames slowly drove the chill from the room and from the house, but not from his core. He paced for a while, then picked up his journal, pulled a rocking chair close to the fire, and still stared outside with his pen in his hand.

He waited for something to change inside him. But the change did not happen. As he had so many times in the past, he began writing, hoping the act of putting painful thoughts and memories into words would make a difference.

About nine, the ice-laced rain turned to real snow. Dane could see it white and ghostly outside the window. He had lived alone for years. Fierce storms no longer alarmed him as they had when he was young. Yet tonight he was uneasy, like a child watching the first foreshadowing scenes of a frightening movie.

The snow fell straight and clean for a while. Then the wind picked up. Snow began to swirl ghostly white curtains across the face of the cold night.

Spirits circled and danced outside the window, discussing this new discovery among themselves, trying to make sense of it. Dewey was there, and Dane's parents, and their parents, and all the Corvins and the Ravens and the rest of the human beings whose chaotic lives had contributed to the genetic mix that became Joshua Hartel.

Even Waldo was there, a burly, sullen presence full of lonely pain and unresolved anger. He glowered across the borderline between life and death, as though he wanted to say something but didn't know the words.

Dane felt the clear presence of the spirits of others in a way that was new to him. They were unsettling reminders of the fragile nature of life and the fleeting impact of a single individual. But they also reminded him that he had come from someplace. He did not exist in a vacuum. He was part of a great chain of beings, each generation caught between the untouchable past and the unknowable future.

Thought. Thought and memory, the twin blessings and the twin curses of mankind.

Twenty years. Twenty years of memories lost. Twenty years of thoughts that were incomplete because Dane didn't know the truth.

The night wore on, and Dane fed more wood into the fire. In

the flickering light, he stared at his son's self-portrait and thought about this strange new being called Josh.

Dane tried to remember all he could from their short phone conversation. The boy was open and honest. That was surprising, since his whole being was based on a lie. Would the truth change his outlook? Would it poison him, as Helen so deeply feared?

Dewey must have wondered about the same thing or he would have told Dane about his suspicions straight out. Dewey was a pragmatist. He had thrown Dane onto a collision course with Josh. But Dewey had not been willing to take the last step. He had not wanted the moral and emotional responsibility for playing God with the truth.

Why? Dane asked the night and himself. What had prevented Dewey? Did he think Josh wasn't ready? Did he think I couldn't confront the truth without destroying something?

The string of questions led back, inevitably, to Helen. Dane tried to sort out the past several weeks, but emotions made it impossible. Truth and lies lay snarled together like discarded threads from a weaver's loom.

He could not separate the first night they made love from the second, the night he lied from the night she misled him in the most breathtaking and heartless way a man could imagine. His own lie was twenty years old, but hers was fresh, as fresh as his sensual memory of being inside her body.

Now everything seemed of a piece, and that piece was shot through with pain and ecstasy, lies and half-truths and finally a full, undeniable truth which shattered everything that came before and changed everything that came after.

Dane grappled with the ghosts of thought and memory for hours, until the fire burned down and the house turned cold again. Finally, he put aside his journal and went to bed.

For the first time since he had moved in, the down comforter was too light to hold back the chill. Toward dawn, the wind switched around and wailed like a banshee straight out of the north.

Dane awoke before first light, cold and cramped. He got up and found a wool blanket to throw across the comforter. Then he lay beneath their combined weight, listening to the wind howl through the trees and around the eaves.

The sun was just rising when Dane got up and looked out. The fall of snow was light. It lay in thin windrows and pale veils on the firs. Leafless shrubs and fallen branches poked lifeless sticks up through the white.

Dane went outside for stove wood. The temperature was twenty-five degrees, and the gusting wind cut through his heavy coat like a sword. He checked to make sure the water pipes were protected. Then he went back in and made a pot of coffee. He spent the rest of the day beside the fire, listening to the wind's contradictions and thinking about his own.

By noon, the storm wind became a gale. It blew directly from the north, attacking trees that had always been sheltered, snapping off leeward branches that had become weak. Deadwood and widow-makers flew through the air and were driven toward the ground like lances.

Twice, Dane heard trees snap and fall in the woods around the house. The trunks made a dry, hollow sound, like breaking bones. He listened with detachment and even toyed with the idea of a walk in the forest. The prospect of dying beneath a falling tree was almost attractive. Death, at least, was final, an end to pain and uncertainty and the relentless savagery of regrets.

The autumn sun had already started toward the southwestern horizon when Dane fixed himself a sandwich from the remnants of a roast. It was the first food he had eaten in more than a day. It tasted good. He made another sandwich, opened a beer, and sat in the rocking chair in front of the wall of windows.

The sweeping fir branches on the nearby trees tossed wildly in the wind. Strands of spray were stripped from the salty waves. The sea seemed full of wrath or a godlike laughter.

Dane set aside his journal, opened another beer, and began prowling Dewey's bookshelves, looking for something that would match his mood, or change it. His hand fell on an old D. H. Lawrence novel he had heard of but never read.

The volume opened easily, as though it had been read many times. Dane scanned a paragraph or two and felt an immediate affinity. He sat down close to the fire and started to read.

He read for almost two hours before the fading November light forced him to choose between the book and the twilight in front of him.

The sky was clear. The blanket of snow magnified the last light. Dane stared into the west until Venus appeared as a clean, yellow-white hole in the dark blue dome of sky.

As he got up to feed the fire once more, the *Wolf and Raven* on the wall above the staircase caught his eye. In the dying light, the raven still seemed to taunt the wolf, but the shadows made both creatures softer.

Dane knew where wolves would go on a night like this. They would den up somewhere out of the wind, cover their paws and noses with their tails, and wait out the blow.

But where, he wondered, does the raven go when the world turns harsh?

Later, Dane turned on a light long enough to make a can of soup and bake a loaf of bread from the freezer. Then he let the fire die down and went to bed again, alone and still without answers.

Dane woke once, at midnight, certain that he had heard a raven call his name. He was a long time getting back to sleep.

SEVENTEEN

A second night of snow had covered the old bones and leafless shrubs. The world was new and clean and very cold. Dane built a fire with the last of his wood, then went out to split some more.

A twisted old fir had fallen close to the garage. The tree's huge trunk and tangled branches formed a barricade across the driveway. Dane walked out along the road in the clear, still air and found three more downed trees between the house and the highway. He was cut off from everyone else.

Dane smiled. Then he laughed, for he finally knew what to do. He went back to the house, fixed himself a working breakfast, and filled a thermos of coffee. Before nine, he had fired up Dewey's chain saw and was trimming limbs off the first fallen tree.

The day was made for work, with clean snow and cold, fresh air. Dane lost himself in the noise of the chain saw, then in the exertion of rolling log rounds off the roadway and stacking cut limbs for burning. As always, he found mental satisfaction and physical release in the demands of hard work. There was a seductive oblivion to it.

By mid-afternoon, Dane was working on the last tree. His eye was caught by the shiny red Cadillac that turned off the highway onto Dewey's road. The big car fishtailed through the rim-deep snow and braked to a stop just short of the last fallen tree. A woman got out.

Dane recognized Irene Tensing, a big woman with shrewd, dark eyes and the moon-shaped face of an aging Indian queen. She wore her heavy shearling coat like a cape and carried a parcel under one arm.

She regarded Dane coldly as she approached. His sweater and woodsman's chaps were coated with fresh sawdust, and his stocking cap was pulled down over his ears. He could have passed for a working lumberjack, and Irene appeared to have had her fill of timber beasts.

"Helen sent this to you," she said, thrusting the parcel in Dane's direction abruptly. "She said you needed it more than she did."

Dane looked at the parcel across the breastwork of the fallen tree, but he did not reach for it.

"What's inside?" he asked coolly. "A bomb?"

"I don't know what's inside, and I don't want to know. I may be an old fool, but I'm smart enough to stay out of this one."

Dane said nothing.

"You realize, don't you," Irene asked, "that you've damned near destroyed her?"

Dane didn't react.

Irene shook the parcel in his direction. "Take it, damn you, and damn all men. Why does it always happen this way?"

"What way is that?" Dane asked with faintly mocking interest.

"I thought you might be good for Helen," Irene said. "She had a light in her eye the other day, talking about you, that gave me some real hope. But then she spent the night with you. She hasn't been the same since. What did you do to her?"

"What do adults usually do when they spend the night together?" Dane asked. "For someone smart enough to stay out of this, you sure ask a lot of dumb questions."

"Listen, you—" Irene bit off the rest of her words. She put the parcel on the fallen log and drew a harsh breath.

Dane smiled like a wolf. "I understand your concern about Helen. You've put a lot of time and planning into her career. Gallery owners are sort of like commodity traders. They make their money cashing in on futures."

Irene studied Dane through narrowed eyes.

"Helen was right," she said. "You can be one cold son of a *bitch.*"

Then Irene looked at Dane more carefully. Beneath his baiting, she sensed the same seething pain she had seen in Helen.

Irene smiled as coldly as Dane had.

"She did get to you, though, didn't she?" Irene asked. "She got you right where it hurts."

Dane didn't answer. Instead, he put down the chain saw, stripped off his gloves, and picked up the parcel. It felt like a book, but was the wrong size. He stripped off the paper wrapping.

It was a photo album. A plain white envelope was taped to the cover.

Irene seemed to recognize the album. Her dark eyebrows rose in surprise. Then she looked at Dane as a man rather than as Helen's enemy. She got as far as his eyes before she shook her head in disbelief and understanding.

"Holy shit," she whispered. She made it sound oddly like a prayer.

"Yeah," Dane agreed. "'Holy shit' just about covers it."

He stared at the album and the envelope, then wrapped it again in the paper and moved it to a clean, dry rock beside the road.

"Thanks for coming by," Dane said, pulling his work gloves back on and picking up the saw. "Just do me a favor. Don't go blabbing your discovery all over town. I'd prefer that Josh heard it from his mother or from me."

"I'm going to do you a favor, Mr. Dane Son of a Bitch Corvin. I'm going to forget you said that."

Irene turned to go back to her car, then stopped.

"Helen asked me to tell you that she just heard from Josh. He'll be flying in Thursday morning. She expects him on the ten o'clock ferry from Langley."

Irene waited for some reaction.

She got none.

"Cold as the north wind, aren't you? How you ever got close enough to Helen to hurt her . . ."

Irene got into her car, slammed the door, and backed it down the road to the highway.

Dane didn't look at the photo album until evening, after he had thawed out in a hot shower and fed himself a hot meal with a bottle of red wine. The house was already dark, so he settled at Dewey's rolltop desk with its good lamp. He slit the white envelope and drew out a single sheet of writing paper.

> *This is a collection of photographs from Josh's life. Some are of him. Others were taken by him.*
> *Study them. Know the boy and young man who is Josh. Then you'll know that Josh isn't as hard as you, wolf. He can be hurt as I was hurt at his age. He can be destroyed as I almost was destroyed at his age.*
> *Remember that Josh is your son, and blameless in all of this. You owe him as much gentleness as you showed to your uncle.*

The note was signed with the elegant outline of a raven in flight, the signature Dane had seen on Helen's works in the gallery.

Dane read the note again, studying the strong, distinctive script, amazed to realize that he had never seen Helen's handwriting before now. There was so much about her he didn't know. He wished he could somehow let that make a difference to him.

Warily, Dane opened the album.

The first picture struck him like the blow from a hammer. Helen stood beneath a fir tree in a light rain, staring out at the open water of Langley Strait. Her face was calm and distant, her eyes thoughtful and dark. Her rounded, pregnant belly pushed out against the buttons of the man's flannel shirt she wore.

She was a beautiful young woman, stark and dignified. She seemed neither happy nor sad. She simply was. She looked into the camera from a distance, as though her physical condition had placed her on the other side of some watershed in human experience.

Dane remembered the words of the old Winomish woman when he had come to Raven Island looking for Helen. Now he realized what the woman had meant. In the picture, Helen was only a few months older than she had been the night she playfully led him to her pine-bough bed.

But she had already become a very different woman. Dane couldn't help wondering how much of the change came from pregnancy and how much from betrayal. Not that he had meant to hurt her. It had simply . . . happened.

No wonder we're so far apart, Dane thought. We went down separate paths a long, long time ago. Does that happen to all men and all women, or just to the ones who can't be honest with each other?

Then he turned the page and encountered a set of pictures of his newborn son. Technically, the pictures were unremarkable, but they brought unexpected tears to Dane's eyes.

Josh a few weeks old, wrapped in a clean, white blanket, his small, round face wrinkled in sleep. The baby nursing at his mother's breast as she stroked his cheek with one long, gracefully curved finger. A bath with the naked baby calm and confident in his mother's grasp.

Dane studied the baby's face. He was no longer a newborn; he had begun to acquire a character of his own.

Then Dane looked at Helen. She looked gaunt, exhausted, as though caring for a baby had turned her into an old woman already. The darkness in her eyes made him uneasy.

No wonder she hated me enough to carry off this little charade, Dane thought. No wonder all women with children view men with some elemental distrust and unresolved anger. Loving a man can have extraordinarily harsh results.

Then Josh, several months old, at what appeared to be a christening. Dane was not a religious man, nor could he easily picture Helen in a church setting. A second picture contained the explanation, Helen and Josh within the comforting circle of a stranger's arm.

Ted Hartel, a big, open-faced man with an air of competent earnestness and decency. He grinned into the camera with a blend of pride and shambling uncertainty that Dane would have found almost amusing, had the woman not been Helen and had the child not been his own.

Instead, Dane felt a cold possessiveness that made him laugh out loud in derision.

That's what she chose? Dane asked silently. A big dumb jughead with a firm faith in God and a salt-of-the-earth manner?

There were several more pages of baby and toddler pictures—Josh grinning and shuffling across a carpet toward his mother's outstretched hands, the boy, dark-eyed and serious in Hartel's lap, reading a picture book.

That snapshot made Dane reassess his first reaction to Hartel. The man was rough-hewn, but straight; a small-town man with little sense of the broader world and less need for it. A terminally decent man.

No kinks, no bends, no flair, but hell, the guy's a fisherman, Dane thought. What did I expect? Somebody with imagination would never tackle the frigid, seventy-foot seas of the Gulf of Alaska in the first place. Hell, he was probably more afraid of Helen than he was of dying.

As for conventional religion, if Christian charity was what motivated Hartel to adopt and raise and love another man's child, Josh had certainly benefited from it. The photos made it painfully clear that Hartel had been an attentive, affectionate father.

Dane looked for Helen in the photos, but didn't find her. All he found was the strong, invisible bond between Hartel and Helen's son. There was a picture of Josh at ten or eleven. It showed hints of adult intelligence in his light eyes and sheer anticipation in his face as he unwrapped a present while Hartel watched with a gentle smile.

Then came another photo dated only a few weeks later. It showed a troubled Josh, withdrawn and sullen and angry, grieving for the man who had raised him as a son.

Part of Dane wanted to dismiss the picture. It was not true, after all. Hartel wasn't Josh's father. But there was no way to deny the anguish in the boy's eyes. Josh's grief had been deep enough to cost a year of school.

There was something unsettling in such passion. Dane reread the note Helen had written, then went back to the photo of Josh. Clearly, Josh had inherited Helen's intense, deep-running emotions—and Waldo's, a lonely man who wanted a connection to life he ultimately found only in heroin and alcohol.

Frowning, Dane turned another page in the photo album. After Hartel's death, there was a change in the snapshots. There were fewer and fewer pictures of Josh and what appeared to be more and more by him.

There was an amateurish portrait of Helen, staring patiently into the lens while her son grappled with the unfamiliar tool called a camera. There were a few landscapes that showed technical proficiency and then one surprisingly evocative shot, a sunset through a cedar grove. The boy had a natural sense of composition.

Gradually, Dane realized that this album Helen had compiled through the years for herself and given to him was unique. There were few pictures of record, few of the obligatory family poses in which the subjects stare and smile blankly into the lens. Instead of the endless cycles of holiday and vacation snapshots, the photos had a subtle, cumulative effect, a feeling of life changing as he watched.

Dane sensed Helen's artistic sense of timing and order in the apparently casual progression of photographs. He studied each page carefully, as though it were a fragment of a big, complex jig-saw puzzle; but in the end, the album resolved nothing except to teach him more of what he already knew: pain. And cruelty. A raven's cruelty, pecking at his eyes until tears came.

It was nearly midnight before he closed the album. The house had grown cold. He wrote in his journal until his hand ached, but there, too, answers eluded him.

That night, Dane dreamed about Josh and Helen and Hartel, satisfied and comfortable with one another, just as they appeared in the album.

Then Dane dreamed that he suddenly appeared on the doorstep. Helen met him and handed him the family album and shut the door.

He opened the book and saw only blank pages.

When Dane awakened the next morning, the rain had returned and melted all the snow. He spent a physical day drag-ging and burning brush and wrestling with wood, but he didn't find the zone of peace. He was haunted by the feeling of loss that had come to him in the dream and had stayed with him through the long day.

He began to fear it would be with him always, like a photo album whose pages were blank.

EIGHTEEN

Helen had just put a twelve-pound turkey into the oven when she heard the knock at the door. Her first thought was that Josh had slipped onto Raven Island ahead of schedule, just to surprise her. She would have been overjoyed at that prospect under other circumstances. Now she was troubled.

She looked out the side window as she wiped her hands on her apron. It was Dane, not Josh, at her front door.

He stood with his back to the door, looking out toward the sunlit water. The photo album was tucked under one arm, and his hands were thrust into the pockets of his coat. His head was bare. His dark hair and beard were trimmed short.

Something, perhaps the fresh haircut, gave Helen the impression of a man who was about to set off on a journey.

She went to the door and opened it. Just beyond Dane's shoulder, she could see the two ravens watching the house from the bare, rough branch of an old fir. The birds were agitated. They hopped up and down nervously, as though awaiting something.

Dane turned at the sound of the door opening. His green eyes were light in the morning sun. His expression was unreadable.

Neither of them spoke.

Helen squared her shoulders and faced him, determined not to let him undermine her confidence with his level stare.

"Josh isn't here yet," she said.

"I didn't come to see Josh." Dane took the album from beneath his arm. "Why did you send this?"

His tone was edged with anger.

Helen started to repeat the message Irene had already delivered. Then she realized how much pain the pictures had inflicted on the man standing before her.

"It wasn't to hurt you," Helen said, her voice husky with subdued emotion. "I meant what I said in the note. I thought you should know Josh, that's all."

Dane considered the response for a moment, then raked his free hand through his hair.

"Don't you believe me?" Helen whispered.

"Oh, hell, yes, I believe you. But for a while there, the first time I went through the album, I thought you were trying to drive me crazy."

"What do you mean?"

"You showed me with cruel artistry just what I had missed. Josh is quite a boy. You and Hartel did a hell of a job raising my son. I suppose I should thank you. Maybe I will, when I can think about it and not want to kill something."

Helen closed her eyes for an instant. Then she opened them and looked levelly at Dane.

"That wasn't what I meant with the album," she said. "It wasn't what I meant at all."

The two ravens dropped off the nearby branch and sailed toward the house, muttering quietly to each other as if annoyed by the people. The bright sun caught on their black feathers, infusing them with a silvery sheen.

Dane watched the birds sail boldly in the chill air. They landed on Josh's rock and waited.

"Do you suppose they know he's coming?" he asked.

"It wouldn't surprise me," Helen replied. She drew a deep breath and squared her shoulders. "What are you going to do, Dane?"

"I want to see my son."

"I can't blame you for that. But what are you going to say to him?"

Dane looked away, unable to meet the fear in her clear black eyes.

"I don't know," he said.

"If you tell him the wrong way, if you drop the truth on him like a brick . . . "

"You don't seem to have much faith in him," Dane said sharply. "If he's as bright as you seem to think, he ought to be able to deal with the truth."

"Truth can be very treacherous. I'd think after what we've gone through, what we've done to each other, you might have figured that out."

"I've survived," Dane shot back, "just like you survived twenty years ago. Sometimes I think the way we turned out wasn't too bad, all things considered.

"Hell, I'm happy with who and what I am," he said with an expansive wave of his hand. "You've done a good job with Josh, and now you're about to take off with a career that will make you famous and probably rich, too.

"We weren't destroyed by truth, were we? What makes you so sure Josh will be?"

Dane glared at Helen with angry fire in his eyes, daring her to dispute his analysis.

"You're right," she said. "We weren't destroyed. *But I can't help thinking what we might have been.*"

Her voice was so soft that Dane couldn't even be sure he had heard correctly. Then he saw the tears that had sprung up in her eyes.

"Goddamn it," Dane growled, angry at himself and at her and at the whole mess called life. "I didn't come here to do another lap around that track."

"Why did you come, then?"

Dane held up the album.

"I wanted to give this back to you, and I wanted to ask you about one of the pictures. I could figure out why you chose most of them, but not this one."

Dane flipped open the album to a photo of Josh at the age of twelve or thirteen. The boy was in swim trunks and standing on what looked very much like the beach in front of the cabin. He was so skinny his ribs showed, but he grinned into the camera and held up a rock the size of a golf ball.

Helen looked at the picture and smiled through her tears. "That's his monster agate. The very first one he ever found, the first one he ever recognized as a special rock."

Dane waited, silently asking to hear more about his son's childhood.

"It was summer, almost a year after Ted died," Helen said. "Josh found the agate right out in front, there beyond the cedar snag. I just happened to have a camera and be with him."

Dane studied the picture again with the new knowledge.

"Josh said something about agates the other day on the phone," Dane said.

Again, Helen sensed the silent question and answered it.

"Agates are his treasure," she said simply. "When he needs his space or time to think, or sometimes even when he's just bored, he heads out to the beach and examines a couple million rocks, looking for the two or three that are agates."

Dane thought about it, then nodded. He found the same kind of space and privacy and sometimes peace in keeping his journal.

"Josh has been over that beach a thousand times since he was thirteen," Helen said. "He and the birds used to pick up every agate they could find."

"Are there any left?" Dane asked, amused by Josh's persistence. That, too, was something Dane could relate to in his unknown son.

"Luckily, each fresh tide brings new ones," Helen said, smiling. "And in the past few years, Josh has gotten a lot more selective. He only keeps the specials."

"We're talking about beach agates, right? Chalcedony, a kind of quartz."

Helen nodded. "You've seen the jar of them in the window."

"Clear beach stones," Dane said. "They don't have any special value, like pearls or coral."

"They do to Josh. He can read more into an agate and get more out it than most people get out of a whole novel. He says they're magic. They help to clarify his thoughts."

Again, Dane thought of his own journal. Wryly, he wondered if agates would have provided a superior form of dialogue with his own mind.

"Magic, huh. Is that what you think?" Dane asked, curious about the mother as much as the son.

"It doesn't matter what I think. Some people meditate on a golf ball, some on a clear quartz crystal, and some on a crucifix. Josh happens to have chosen beach agates. If you have a problem with that, blame me. I encouraged him."

"I wasn't being critical. I was just trying to figure out what Josh sees in them."

"He says they give off more light than they take in."

"He's a dreamer, isn't he?"

"There are worse things to be," Helen said.

"You were a dreamer once."

"And you weren't." Swiftly Helen held up her hand. "I'm sorry. Let's not get into it all over again. It's in the past, and the future arrives on the next ferry."

Dane looked down at the album again.

"If you want to know your son better," Helen said softly, "go down on the beach and look for agates. There's plenty of time before the ferry."

Dane glanced doubtfully toward the beach. "I wouldn't have the faintest idea what to look for."

"Just look for the rocks that give off more light than they absorb," she said, smiling gently. "Take Thought and Memory. They'll help you."

Dane took a step toward the water, then hesitated as though he suspected Helen was trying somehow to trick him.

"Go ahead. I'll let you know when it's time to go," she said.

Dane looked around, surprised at her implicit suggestion. "Do you think that's a good idea to go together?"

"I don't know if it's a good idea, but I know I won't let you meet him alone."

An hour later, Dane had studied more scattered beach rocks at the water's edge than he could count. No agates had appeared for him. The ravens had been nearby the whole time, wary and skittish and wise and wild.

They leaped into the air and sailed off on the breeze to circle around Helen as she approached. She wore her cape loosely fastened at her throat and drawn over her shoulders. She was dressed in dark slacks and a deep green sweater; a strong, willowy, attractive woman who did not look old enough to be the mother of a boy on the edge of manhood.

Once more, Dane tasted the bitter legacy of his lie and hers. Helen was still the most desirable woman he had ever known, and she had borne him a fine, strong, worthy son.

But both she and Josh were beyond his reach, part of a past that couldn't be changed.

"Any luck?" Helen asked, her voice neutral, guarded.

Dane shook his head. She stopped a few feet away, close enough that he could catch her scent. She was fresh and clean, like lavender soap.

The ravens had settled onto the sandy ground at the high-tide line. There they sat, watching the humans. Helen glanced toward them.

"Didn't Thought and Memory give you any help?" she asked.

"They landed a couple of times and hopped around like kangaroos, but I couldn't see what they were getting upset about."

"I think they were trying to tell you to keep the rock beds

between yourself and the sun," Helen said. "That's the best way to see agates."

She walked to where the tide was receding and squinted back up the beach into the sun.

"Other kinds of quartz are translucent when they are wet," she said. "The beach is loaded with them.

"But only agate stays as shiny when it is dry. Only agate casts a colored shadow. Only agate overflows with light."

Helen walked along for a few yards, looking back toward Dane and the birds, which were hopping up and down.

"Actually, the ravens are trying to tell you about an agate," Helen said, squinting into the light. "I think there's one right there."

She pointed to a windrow of smallish pebbles a few yards in front of Dane. He went forward slowly, studying the rocks that were still slick with water.

"Come around to this side," Helen said. "Let the sun do the work."

Dane circled the low bank of rubble. Suddenly a rock the size of his thumb blazed with rich, brown-orange light. He reached down and scooped it up with an odd feeling of triumph. When he held the rock between himself and the sun, the stone shimmered and changed before his eyes.

The effect was startling. The rock became almost transparent. Part of the agate was blue-white like a moonstone; the other part looked like a solid chunk of bitter-orange marmalade with strings of rind suspended gracefully within.

The ravens sprang into the air and circled around Dane, gronking happily, as though to congratulate him and to claim part of the credit for the find.

"Wow," Dane said.

"Zowie," Helen said.

He gave her a sideways look.

"That's what Josh says when he finds a good one," Helen said, smiling. "Let me see."

She took the agate and held it up to the light.

"That's a 'zowie,' all right. Congratulations. You'll never be able to look at a beach the same way again. There will always be that . . . "

"That what?"

"That one-in-a-million chance of unexpected beauty."

Dane looked at the woman and then at the agate in his hand.

"Too bad life isn't an agate hunt," he said after a time.

"But it is," she countered softly. "That's what Josh and his ravens taught me."

Dane was silent for a moment, thinking. He started to say something, but Helen cut him off sharply, as though their talk had strayed into dangerous territory again.

"We'd better hurry," Helen said. "The ferry is due in twenty minutes."

NINETEEN

The choppy waters of the channel caught the sky's blue brilliance and turned it dark and moody. The last autumn warmth was locked in unfair battle with the winter wind.

Dane sat in his truck, listening to the whistling wind and watching the green-and-white Washington state ferry beat across the open channel, bringing with it his inevitable choice. In five minutes, three lives would be changed, and he wasn't sure whether he was ecstatic or desolate or simply foolish.

Woman or son. Once he might have had both. Now he would have to settle for one, and even that one was uncertain. It would be very easy for Josh to hate the messenger, especially if Helen encouraged it. The stark facts of seduction and betrayal and abandonment were enough to make Dane wince, and he was a lot harder than Josh.

The fact that Helen had a full part in all of it could easily be overlooked by a loving son.

Still, Helen seemed to draw no comfort from her advantage. Clearly, she was terrified of losing Josh. She knew all too well what happened when a dreamer's life was broken into a thousand sharp pieces.

Christ in heaven, Dane thought. What a mess.

He got out and stood beside the truck, feeling the knife edge of coming winter in the wind.

Another year gone by, he thought bitterly. Another set of chances lost. A startling chance discovered. A last chance, too. I'm past the point where I can—or will—start over with any woman.

God, but that is a steep price to pay for a simple lie of love.

Helen arrived in her own car and parked beside Dane's truck. She watched the incoming ferry as though it bore her executioner. Then she glanced out through the windshield and caught a glimpse of Dane's wolf-green eyes. Blank and unreadable, they told her nothing.

In that one glance, Dane became the wary wolf in her wood carving. He showed nothing of himself but a feral alertness and the flash of a cool green eye.

What a poor raven I've been for my wolf, she thought. What a failure as a guide. We allied ourselves. Then he betrayed me and I deserted him. Now he'll starve for want of love.

But I'll pay, too. Again. Foolish raven. After today, my son will never again look at me with trust. I can survive that, I guess. My greatest fear is that Josh will never trust anything human again, that he will never learn wisdom from a child of his own, that he will be a wolf forever without his raven.

Helen would have cried, but she didn't dare let go her control that much. She would have pleaded, but pleas would not change the truth. Nor would they change Dane's need for a son.

So Helen did the only thing she could do. She got out and stood in the cold wind, watching the ferry loom larger and larger every second.

Dane stood ten feet away, on the other side of her car. He studied the incoming ferry as though he was trying to memorize every detail, anchoring himself in the mundane. The boat was double-ended, with two car decks and a high pilothouse. The long, flat masts of the onboard radar turned mindlessly, redundant in the bright sunlight. Dane could see the walk-on passengers gathering behind the chain railing on the main deck. They were still too far away to make out faces.

"Is he aboard?" Dane asked tightly.

Helen nodded. "There on the right side, just behind the chains. He always wants to be the first one off."

Dane strained to see. A group of people had gathered in the spot Helen indicated. A dark head of hair caught his eye, sticking out above a spot of red and several baseball caps.

"He's taller than I expected," Dane said.

Helen had to remind herself to breathe.

"Six feet one, probably more now," she said softly. "He was still growing when he left home."

There was a wistfulness in Helen's voice that drove a rusty nail into Dane's heart.

"If you can think of some way to make this easier for you, I will," he said.

Helen smiled sadly. "Compassion from a wolf. As unexpected as an agate on a beach full of ordinary stones." She drew a deep, ragged breath. "Thank you, Dane, but no. There is nothing. . . ."

The ferry pilot turned the broad open nose of the boat upwind a few degrees to compensate for the drift. The black plume that spewed out of the exhaust stack shrank as the pilot reduced power and slowed, trying to match forward momentum with inertia.

The figures behind the barrier in the bow were close enough to make out separate faces, individual features. Dane was stunned at the recognition that flooded through him. He would have known Josh as his son, even if Helen had not pointed him out.

The tall youth in the blue Gore-Tex parka bounced up and down on his toes eagerly. He waved when he recognized his mother. She waved back and started walking slowly toward the open gangway that led up from the dock.

Dane hung back, faintly disappointed. The boy hadn't even given him a second look.

Helen stopped and waited for Dane. "He's not expecting you, that's all," she said.

Dane shoved his hands into the pockets of his coat and went after her. His fingers found the cool, oily-smooth agate, and he grabbed it, rubbing it slowly, like a worry stone.

"Scared?" Helen asked when he joined her.

Dane nodded, surprised that she had recognized his fear before he had.

"Good," she said. "Wolves are careful when they're scared."

They arrived at the head of the gangway just as the ferry slid into the shelter of the heavy timber wing walls. Josh was bareheaded. The wind caught his dark hair and pulled it aside, giving him a wild handsomeness that was startling.

"He hasn't gotten it cut since September," Helen said. Her voice was a mixture of parental pride and dismay.

"He looks fine. Every man should grow his hair long once in his life, to see whether he likes it that way."

Helen looked at Dane quickly. For a few seconds, the tension between them eased.

"I didn't know men were so vain," she said teasingly.

Dane smiled but didn't reply.

The nose of the ferry slid slowly into the slot between the wing walls, spending the remainder of its momentum in a perfect landing. But at the last moment, a gust of wind caught the broad flank of the boat and pushed it sideways. Inexorably, inevitably, the massive boat slewed toward the leeward wall, missing the berth by a couple of feet.

After a moment of indecision, the pilot of the ferry tapped his bow thrusters and backed off slowly, trying to angle the ponderous boat back into its slot.

Josh was first in line to debark. He watched the slow-motion ballet with sudden, unquenchable impatience. As the ferry slid off its mark, the young man impulsively peeled the pack off his shoulder and stepped over the chain barrier.

Helen sensed her son's intentions instantly. He had leaped ashore from the ferry before. He regarded it as harmless fun, in part because it terrified her so.

"No, Josh!" she called out.

It was too late. Josh tossed the pack across the yard-wide gap to the landing ramp. Then he gathered himself to follow. The gap was now five feet wide and getting wider with every second.

Dane felt an extraordinary and unaccustomed surge of protectiveness as he saw his son prepare to leap from the bow of the ferry to the steel plate of the ramp.

Waves had splashed the ramp. Dane recognized instantly that it would be slippery and treacherous.

The dark water beneath the bow of the boat boiled as the thrusters and screws fought for control. Slowly, the three-thousand-ton ferry moved forward.

"Jesus," Dane said softly.

It was a prayer. If Josh missed and went into the water, he could be drawn under by the boil, chopped up by the bronze propellers, or crushed against the twelve-inch-square timbers.

Dane and Helen held their breaths and waited for what seemed like an hour but was only a fraction of a second. Josh shifted his stance on the slippery deck and prepared to leap. Then a striking young woman with dark auburn hair and a serious expression reached across the chains and touched Josh's arm.

The young man turned, grinned wickedly, and said something to the young woman. She looked worried and shook her head.

Josh's exuberant expression changed to concern. He touched the girl's cheek in a gesture that could have been reassurance or apology or both at once. The smile she gave him in return was the kind that could light up a lifetime of nights.

As the gap between the ferry and the ramp opened even more, Josh took the girl's hand and folded it inside his own. Then he glanced in his mother's direction, shrugged sheepishly, and let the girl lead him back across the chains to the safety of the deck.

Helen stared at the sight of her reckless young wolf tamed by a female whose favor he obviously sought.

In that instant, Helen knew that Josh had crossed over a critical watershed. She felt a sharp stab of pain and loss, and simultaneously knew a rush of joy and satisfaction. Josh was a young male with a loving soul. He needed a young female with an equally loving nature.

What Helen had seen of Josh and the girl with the auburn hair suggested that he had found himself a mate, and so had she.

"Well, well, well," Dane said, smiling slightly. "From the looks of it, Josh is bringing his Christmas surprise home a few weeks early. And quite a surprise it is."

Silently, Helen watched as the ferry pilot struggled to swing his heavy craft around and return it to the slip. Her mind seemed to be on fire as she tried to absorb the changed relationship between herself and her son.

Suddenly, Helen laughed out loud with joy.

Dane looked at her uncertainly. Her face was alight. The sun caught the silvery highlights of her lustrous black hair.

"What's so funny?" Dane asked cautiously.

"Nothing."

Then Helen laughed aloud again. The sound was like music.

"We both just got a lesson in letting go," she said. "I've been clinging to my son with all my might, protecting him. You've been searching for him, whether you knew it or not, trying to find your own antidote to mortality through him."

Helen laughed softly.

"And all the while," she said, "Josh was already beyond our reach. Now he belongs to that young woman out there."

"For a while," Dane said skeptically.

"Forever is a while."

Dane looked at Helen.

"You can tell just by looking at him?" he asked, but there was curiosity rather than doubt in his tone.

"I can tell by looking at *her*."

Dane stared at Helen, then laughed like a wolf. Together, they watched the couple on the deck of the ferry. Josh stood with his arm around the young woman's shoulders, proud and protective and a little defiant, as though he still wasn't sure how to tell his mother about the startling change in his life.

The girl stood securely within the strength of Josh's arm. Her own arm was around his waist, as though she was providing some subtle support for him. The boat was close enough that she could see Helen clearly.

Dane watched as a wordless communication passed between the women. Helen smiled encouragingly, and the girl smiled back.

Then the young woman looked at Dane. He sensed both her intelligence and her excitement as she studied his face. Her expression changed for an instant, surprise or something else. She turned her head and said something to Josh.

Josh looked at Dane for a second and shrugged, as though Josh might have agreed or disagreed with whatever the girl had said. But before the conversation could continue, the ferry slipped into its berth and came to rest delicately against the wing walls. A deckhand stationed himself in front of the debarking passengers while the steel ramp from the dock was lowered into place.

"Dane," Helen said quickly, "I have to say something before they get here."

Reluctantly, Dane took his eyes off his son's face and turned to Helen. She was facing him, her eyes intense with a mixture of emotions.

One of them was hope.

"Go ahead," Dane said.

"I lied," Helen said starkly. "Not to you, at least not directly, but to myself. I just realized, this moment, that my son wasn't the only reason I couldn't tell you the truth."

Dane stared at her silently, waiting for the rest of it. He held his breath, knowing this was the last chance either one of them would have before Josh and girl arrived.

"I couldn't tell you the truth because I was afraid you would finally and forever hate me," Helen said in a voice that was both calm and strained. "I was trying to protect myself, not Josh."

Dane stood silently, his fists jammed in the pockets of his coat. He seemed to hear Helen's words with the inner ear of memory, as though they were words he once had spoken himself.

"You told me once that you knew what a person would do for love," she said. "So do I. Now. They will lie, even to themselves."

Dane swallowed hard and slowly took his hands from his pockets. He opened his right palm, revealing the translucent stone the two ravens had pointed out on the beach. Clear sunlight shot through the agate and made it glow. Dane shifted his palm and let the stone roll over, catching the light and shooting it back at them like a bursting star.

Then he held out his hand, offering the stone to Helen. His voice was as soft as it had been their first night in the forest.

"It's hard enough for us to forgive ourselves and each other, Helen. I'm not going to put that burden on Josh, not right now, when he has just found his mate. I want him to have a better chance at love than we did."

Helen blinked against the tears she shouldn't cry.

"You do know about being a father, after all," she whispered.

With fingers that trembled faintly, Helen touched the stone in Dane's hand. Very gently, he closed his fingers over hers.

"I'll leave if you want," he said simply, "or stay if you want. Either way, I won't destroy Josh's memories of the past and his thoughts of the future. He already has one father. That's plenty. I know I have a son."

"Is that enough for you?" Helen asked.

Dane hesitated. "It's more than I ever expected."

"He might guess the truth."

"I doubt it," Dane said. "Ask any cop—people see what they expect to see. Josh doesn't expect to see a father when he looks at me."

"Whatever happens," Helen said, "I've been too long without you. Stay with me. Let me love you. And . . . love me if you can."

Dane's hand tightened almost painfully around hers. Then he pulled Helen into his arms and held her, simply held her as though he would never let her go. She held him just as tightly in return.

They were still in each other's arms when a young wolf and a young raven appeared at the top of the ramp and stood watching, surprised to see that they weren't the only male and female in the world to have discovered the possibility of love.

EPILOGUE

As I read Dane's journal this week, the memory of that day came back to me as vividly as an agate in the sun. But now, as I sit in the cabin in Denali, I remember even more clearly what Eileen said to me as the ferry docked.

"He looks a *lot* like you. Tall and handsome and kind of wild."

"Who?" I asked.

"The man standing next to your mother."

That was the first time I saw Dane Corvin. Like most of us, I seldom see myself as others do, so I had to take Eileen's word about my resemblance to Dane. Besides, I was trying to figure out what I was going to say to my mother, how I was going to introduce the woman I knew I someday would marry.

I liked Dane right away for the smile he had put on my mother's face and the light in her eyes. I never had reason to change my opinion of him, not in all the years since that Thanksgiving morning.

But I never asked him, directly or indirectly, if he was my father.

I think Eileen must have guessed the truth, though she never said anything to me. She loved both my mother and Dane too much to hurt them. She and Dane were especially close. Eileen was so happy when our daughter, Danielle, who is now four, was born with the green eyes that Eileen tells me are my strength.

Wolf's eyes, my mom called them. And she looked at Dane when she spoke.

Until that moment four years ago, when I realized my child's eyes were so much like Dane's, I had never questioned whether Ted Hartel was my father. Later, I was tempted to bring it up, but I always decided against it.

As the saying goes, *If it works, don't fix it.*

For Dane and me, it worked. Today, I am a professional wildlife photographer, and any success I achieve is a result of his help. He had an incredible knowledge of wild animals, of where they would be, and when, and why. He taught me when to be patient and when to throw my head back and howl at the moon like a wolf.

With Dane's help, I took a series of photos of Alaskan wolves that has helped to change the public view of the animals. Wolves are now more understood and more valued. Eventually, I hope they will be celebrated and protected rather than harassed and executed.

I never asked my mother about the uncanny match between Dane's eyes and mine and Danielle's. I didn't want to hurt Mom or Dane. They were good for each other. Until I saw her with Dane, I didn't know how much of my mother had been missing, like a raven with clipped wings, forced to walk where it would have flown. I can only assume it was the same for Dane, that Mom strengthened him as much as she freed her.

God knows, Dane was strong in all the ways that count for a man. Physically tireless, mentally alert, unafraid of emotion. The first time he held little Danielle, he had tears in his eyes. He was always patient with her, even when Eileen and I were fed up with her persistence and her fey teasing. Dane couldn't have loved Dani more if she had been his own blood.

Now I know that she was.

Now I hold the proof in my hands, a family album and a journal that tells me how cruelly my mother and Dane struggled for the love they finally attained.

I try not to cry for them. They wouldn't have wanted it. They don't need it. Yet I cry, because I am alive and they are not.

Six months ago, in the Arctic's high spring, Mother and Dane took off in a small plane to search for one of the migrating wolf-packs. They never returned. Their remains have never been found. I hope they never will be.

On the table in front of me, Dane's journal is open to a page where he copied a passage from a novel, *Lady Chatterley's Lover*, by D. H. Lawrence. The words are taken from a letter written by a man to the woman he loves:

> *Patience, always patience. This is my fortieth winter. And I can't help all the winters that have been. But this winter I'll stick to my little Pentecost flame, and have some peace. And I won't let the breath of people blow it out. I believe in a higher mystery, that doesn't let even the crocus be blown out. And if you're in Scotland and I'm in the Midlands, and I can't put my arms round you, and wrap my legs round you, yet I've got something of you. My soul softly flaps in the little Pentecost flame with you, like the peace of fucking. We fucked a flame into being. Even the flowers are fucked into being between the sun and the earth. But it's a delicate thing and takes patience and the long pause.*

I understand the passage because I have read the entire book. It answers many questions I never asked of Dane and Mother.

But it doesn't tell me what to say to my own green-eyed child, or how great the patience must be, and how long the pause, and how to live at peace with the twin ravens of thought and memory.

Evan Maxwell, working often with his wife, Ann, is the author of more than forty-five books, both fiction and nonfiction. Using several pen names, he and his wife have collaborated on mysteries, romantic adventures, and *New York Times* best-selling historical romances. He and Ann live in the San Juan Islands of Washington.